GRIPPED
part 1

GRIPPED PART 1
THE TRUTH
WE NEVER
TOLD

Written by Stacy A. Padula
Edited by Michael Mattes

Briley & Baxter Publications | Plymouth, Massachusetts

ISBN: 978-1-7350168-3-2

Book Design: Amy Deyerle-Smith

Dedicated to Timothy O'Halloran

MAIN CHARACTER
BACKGROUND INFORMATION

Taylor Dunkin

Taylor grew up as the acclaimed hometown hero of Montgomery, Massachusetts. He was very close with his parents and his younger brothers, Marc and Jordan. He was praised by his classmates and teachers and heavily recruited for Division I football. He was committed to attend the University of Notre Dame until he was arrested during his senior year of high school. Although his arrest was the result of being in the wrong place at the wrong time, Taylor lost his chance with ND, which resulted in him feeling a tremendous amount of shame. He walked onto Northeastern University's notoriously struggling football team and helped them turn things around. As a sophomore, he was ranked by ESPN as an NFL Top Prospect. However, he tore his ACL, MCL, and both menisci during an early season game that left him sidelined for his senior season. After two surgeries, he developed a dependence on Percocet.

Marc Dunkin

Marc is Taylor's youngest brother: a strait-laced, good kid with lofty goals and principles. He grew up in the shadow of Taylor and Jordan, who both have a bit more natural athletic talent than Marc. However, Marc works extra hard at everything he does and seems to always succeed. Blessed with the good looks and a charismatic personality, Marc is a popular kid—especially with girls. However, his focus is on fitness, academics, and his family. Marc has a close relationship with Taylor, whom he grew up admiring. After trying for months to get Taylor to go to rehab, he learns that Taylor has been dealing drugs to his own best friend, Luke Davids. Suddenly, the drug problem amongst teens in Montgomery makes sense.

Cathy Kagelli

Cathy is an identical twin, who grew up in a Christian home. She was sheltered from the evils of the world by her parents, who are loving, understanding, and devoted to their children. Her outgoing twin sister, Chantal, was her best friend until they had a falling out in middle school. After Chantal cut ties with her, Cathy began experiencing intense bouts of anxiety and depression that led her to begin self-medicating.

Chris Dunkin

Chris is the younger cousin of Taylor, Jordan, and Marc, known by his friends as "the life of the party." Like his cousins, Chris is an elite athlete, perhaps as naturally talented as Taylor. Chris grew up with minimal support at home. A nanny raised him and his younger sister Katie because his parents traveled abroad for their business for weeks at a time. When Chris entered middle school, his parents began leaving Taylor and Jordan in charge of their home whenever they traveled, which exposed Chris to high school and college parties at the ripe age of thirteen.

Jason Davids

Jason has been Chris Dunkin's best friend since Kindergarten. He attended a prestigious Catholic school from first through eighth grade. Jason has not earned lower than an A in a class since fourth grade; his IQ is above 140; and he is a perfectionist to a fault. However, he constantly needs mental stimulation or he gets bored, which usually translates to experimenting with things he shouldn't.

Luke Davids

Luke is Jason's kind, people-pleasing, and gregarious older brother, who ends up being the liaison between Taylor and kids in Montgomery who want to buy drugs. In Luke's mind, he is not a drug dealer because he makes no money off the sales; he is just doing people favors by getting them what they want.

PREFACE

To Readers Across America:

Each day, more and more young adults fall prey to substance abuse. As an educator who works mainly with high school students, I was moved to write a book series for teenagers that shares how it happens—how good kids become drug addicts, how downward spirals start, how harmless fun can quickly turn into a life-threatening addiction.

The story told in the series is raw and realistic. I did not censor much of the content, for I believe the truth is important and powerful. In our world in which twelve-year-old kids overdose in middle school bathrooms, it is time for authors to stop sugarcoating their content to appease schoolboards. I am aware that this book may be banned by public schools because of the harsh realities portrayed between its covers. However, I did not write any part of the *Gripped* book series in hopes of it being taught in English classrooms. The truth is far too controversial for that, even though the events depicted in *Gripped* happen daily across America.

The series portrays the story of Taylor Dunkin who was an acclaimed college athlete, seemingly destined for the NFL but sidelined by injury. His depression leads him to begin abusing his pain medication and eventually become a drug dealer to support his habit. He supplies drugs to high school students from his hometown, which leads to other characters becoming ensnared. The story shows how drug abuse can skew individuals' values and change their perspectives. It follows other characters such as Luke Davids, Cathy Kagelli, Chris Dunkin, and Jason Davids (also featured in my *Montgomery Lake High* book series) whose lives have been affected by Taylor's decisions. It shows the psychological, biological, and environmental reasons behind why people often begin experimenting with drugs and how slippery the slope can be. Most importantly, this book series educates readers on how people can pick up the pieces of their lives and recover from such a horrific epidemic.

I have written five other young adult novels that address teenage social issues. They comprise the *Montgomery Lake High* book series. Over the past eleven years, the books have frequently been on the Amazon top 100 best seller list for young adult books that address substance abuse. In the fall of 2017, four of the books were top 10 best sellers within the category. Considering the sharp rise in prescription drug overdoses and opiate abuse, I feel that the *Gripped* book series is needed now more than ever. Please join me in helping to protect the youth from opiate and benzodiazepine abuse by recommending Gripped to a teenager you know.

Sincerely,
Stacy A. Padula

PROLGUE

Marc Dunkin

Community is strange. It's amazing and necessary but strange. It's probably just the way I look at it, but whenever I hear the word, I imagine this big elaborate shape—not a real shape, at least not according to geometry class, but a bunch of lines, dots, and circles. Again, it's strange, I know.

The circle in the middle is my family: Mom, Dad, Taylor, Jordan, and me. Even though each of us is spread equally around the ring, I still imagine that if one of us had to be at the center, it would be Taylor.

That's where the lines come in. They connect us to other people (dots) and groups (circles). Taylor, well, he draws them wherever he goes. Taylor has something about him that makes everyone gravitate towards him. It drives me insane that I respect him as much as I do, but I just can't help it.

For years, Taylor was unstoppable—destined for greatness, on and off the field—until he was literally and figuratively blindsided. Despite having a family history of addiction, we all underestimated the grip of opiates. It didn't seem possible that someone as smart, driven, and conscientious as Taylor could fall victim to addiction. Taylor was on our pedestal, and we were blind to his weaknesses.

Prior to his injury, there were warning signs we missed, signs that he was buckling under the pressure he placed upon himself to be perfect, to carry his team, and to make our family proud. With so many eyes on him all the time, it is ironic that no one actually saw him, his struggles, or his pain. They saw his glory, the larger than life figure he was, and the moral person he used to be before college.

Taylor fell hard, and his fall impacted people beyond our immediate circle. *Everything* is connected in the <u>Gripped</u> book series—the circles, the dots, the lines. Most notable are the powdery lines that link Taylor to my best friend, Luke Davids, and Luke to my love interest, Cathy Kagelli. As the books progress (and Taylor and Cathy's stories start to merge), you'll see that some lines we draw just can't be erased...

CHAPTER 1

November 2017

M ARC DUNKIN PARKED HIS red Dodge truck on South Huntington Avenue and turned off the engine. He was not ready to go inside his oldest brother Taylor's apartment. Even though he had spent the half-hour drive from Montgomery to Boston ruminating over the situation, he felt ill-prepared for the ensuing conversation.

Taylor, who had been addicted to painkillers for over a year, was blazing a trail of destruction. Even though Taylor was technically alive, he was nearly dead to Marc. The conscientious and driven role model Taylor had always been no longer existed. He was a shell of the athlete Marc grew up admiring.

Marc was lost in thought as he climbed out of his truck. A moment later, he stood at Taylor's front door, knocking loudly. A minute went by without any response. He sent a text message to Taylor but received no reply. It was close to one o'clock, and they had planned to watch football together all day. Marc tried calling Taylor's cell phone, but it went straight to voicemail. At that point, Marc's heart started pounding against his muscular chest, and he feared the worst. He had been trying for months to save his brother from a downward spiral.

Standing on Taylor's porch, Marc took a deep breath. He turned the doorknob, but of course it was locked. He felt above the door and looked below the mat for a spare key but found nothing. It was November, so the windows were shut and locked. Marc remembered that his parents kept a key taped under their porch's banister, and he hoped Taylor did the same. After thirty seconds of searching, he found the key he was petrified to turn.

"Hello?" Marc called while entering Taylor's apartment. All was still. To his dismay, he could not hear the shower running, and the TV was off. *Most people would think their brother was just hungover and still sleeping,* Marc thought. *I have to worry about finding him dead.*

"Taylor?" Marc cried out loudly as he walked through the living room toward Taylor's bedroom. After banging on his bedroom door a few times and getting no response, Marc barged into the room. The room-darkening shades were drawn, and Marc had to turn on the light to see if Taylor was in his bed. He was wrapped up in his comforter, lying on his side in the fetal position.

"T, wake up! It's almost game time," Marc stated loudly.

No response.

Slowly Marc walked over to the bedside and observed his brother. *At least he's still breathing.* Turning to the window, Marc opened the shades and allowed sunlight to fill the room. "Time to get up, T," he said as he turned back toward the bed. He sat down on the edge of it and nudged his brother.

Taylor let out a slight moan but continued sleeping.

"Get up, dude," Marc demanded, nudging him again. No matter how hard he shook him, he could not get Taylor to acknowledge his presence. It was like he was in a trance.

Marc felt dejected as he sat and looked around Taylor's room. He leaned toward the nightstand and opened the top drawer. Sure enough, it was filled with prescription bottles: Xanax, Percocet, Klonopin, and OxyContin—Taylor's favorite. Marc picked up the OC bottle and noticed it was empty. Years prior, pharmaceutical companies had stopped producing the extended-release, crushable tablets that Taylor liked to snort, so OxyContin was difficult to come by—even for someone as well-connected as Taylor. This scared Marc because he knew his brother was dependent on it.

Marc shut the drawer and looked for any traces of powder on his nightstand. There was a residue, but it wasn't white. Marc squinted and tried to figure out what his brother had snorted. He whipped open the bottom drawer of the nightstand to find a large green box. After opening it up, Marc found himself staring at a large quantity of marijuana, small bags of cocaine, an unmarked bag of small blue pills, a large bag of smiley-face-embossed ecstasy, a bag of capsules that were likely filled with molly, and an unlabeled vial of a yellowish powder.

Marc darted his eyes at Taylor and then back at the green box. He sat in complete shock, realizing the vial could be filled with heroin. His heart pounded. He glanced again at the residue on the nightstand. It was so sparse that he couldn't tell what color it was. "T, wake up, buddy," Marc said again and nudged his brother hard in the back.

"What's up?" Taylor mumbled without opening his eyes or flinching.

"The Pats game is on. Time to get up."

"I'm good," he mumbled.

Marc sighed and stood up from the bed. As he did, he heard something crack beneath his shoe. Lifting his foot revealed a small pile of broken plastic. Marc's throat went immediately dry, and he felt the color drain from his face. He was faint at the realization he had just stepped on an empty vial, one that most likely had been filled with the yellowish powder. He walked out of Taylor's bedroom in a daze. It took a minute, but the tears came, and they didn't stop until halftime.

CHAPTER 2

LATER THAT AFTERNOON, MARC widened his blue eyes when he heard Taylor's bedroom door squeak open. After hours alone with his thoughts, he still had no idea what to say.

"I'm *so* sorry, dude," Taylor said as he entered the room. "I totally forgot you were coming over for the game. How did you get in?"

"Your spare key," Marc replied, unable to look at his brother as he lay down on the couch across from him.

"Under the banister just like at home," Taylor said lightheartedly.

"Dude, what the hell were you just on?" Marc asked and shot Taylor a look of panic.

Taylor was wrapping himself up in a blanket; his coloring looked terrible. "I'm sick," he replied. He pulled the hood of his gray sweatshirt over his messy blonde hair and locked his blue eyes on the TV.

"Well, what did you do? Take too much Nyquil? You were in a trance."

"You don't want to hear about it," Taylor stated flatly, holding his gaze on the television.

"No. I *do* want to hear about it," Marc said sternly.

Taylor sighed. "I ran out of OCs, and I'm going through withdrawal."

"You didn't look withdrawn."

Taylor groaned and turned toward Marc. "I couldn't sleep last night. My heart was racing, and I kept puking. Finally, around eight this morning, I crushed up some Percocet and Xanax. The mixture knocked me out, but now

I feel like death."

The Xanax Marc saw in Taylor's drawer was yellow. He wondered if the vial he had found was, in fact, filled with a Percocet/Xanax combination. Knowing all Taylor knew about drugs, he must have been desperate to mix Percocet and Xanax together. Mixing opiates and benzos was a quick recipe for an overdose. "What are you doing to yourself?" Marc asked and shook his head disgustedly. "Go to rehab."

"I don't have insurance," Taylor said. "Mom and Dad cut me from the policy when I stopped talking to them."

"They know there's more going on with you than depression. If you ask them for help, they'll reinstate you. They'd pay anything to help you."

"What do they know?"

"I told them you're taking too many painkillers and you need rehab. They didn't believe me until you stopped coming home or taking their calls."

"I can't let Dad see me like this," Taylor said quietly. "I'm sorry, dude, but can we just watch the game? I can't deal with this conversation right now."

"Well, we need to have another conversation."

"What?"

"How long have you been supplying Luke with drugs?"

Taylor's blue eyes widened.

"How long?"

Taylor sat up straight and looked away from Marc. "Long enough."

Marc's heart sank. "Shoot straight with me. What's he into?"

"Luke? Molly and coke."

"Then why is he giving painkillers to his little brother?"

"To Jason? I don't know," Taylor replied defensively. "Probably because he doesn't want them and Jason does."

"So, he sells for you in Montgomery?"

"No!" Taylor exclaimed. "Luke's been buying drugs from me all year. He gets a good amount every time, so I assume he's distributing. Who he gives them to is none of my business."

"You used to babysit us!" Marc cried in dismay. "Why would you sell him drugs?"

"I can't deal with this right now," Taylor whined. "I'm sorry. I feel like $@%&."

"Before Chris went straightedge, he almost OD'd because he drank on Xanax and Vicodin that he got from Luke. Those drugs came from *you*. Our cousin could have died because of *you*."

"I didn't tell Chris to do that," Taylor retorted.

"When you give pills to Luke, he gives them to kids we know. *Why* would you do that?"

"Marc, what do you want me to say?"

"I want you to realize how much damage you are causing in the lives of people you once cared about. I want you to stop blowing things up your nose and re-apply to college. Do you know how many schools would want you if they knew your knee was healed? You could go anywhere you wanted, and you could be on a sick team. You belong at 'Bama or Auburn or Notre Dame with Jordan. Dad could even make a call to The U."

"I can't deal with this," Taylor said and rolled over on his side.

"You know what I can't deal with? Any of this!" Marc exclaimed and stood up from the couch. "I'm done. I love you more than anyone, bro. You were my idol for seventeen years of my eighteen years on earth, but I'm done."

A moment later, Marc stormed out of Taylor's apartment. As soon as he reached his truck, he called his father. "Dad, you have to come to Boston and talk to Taylor."

"Where are you?"

"I just left his place. I took his spare key."

"What happened?"

"He ran out of his painkillers, and he's going through withdrawal. He needs rehab," Marc replied, feeling himself start to choke up. "I'll tell you the rest when I get home. I have to drive, and I'm too upset to talk."

Marc hung up the phone and took a deep breath. He felt like his world was crashing down. He could not bear the thought of Taylor mixing benzos and opiates to ease his withdrawal symptoms. It was a deadly concoction... and if *that* wasn't what he had taken, then he had snorted heroin. Either scenario was terrifying.

When Marc returned home, both of his parents were waiting for him. Marc's father was a recovered alcoholic who had been sober for fifteen years. Marc grew up attending Al-Anon meetings with his mother and brothers, so he knew a lot about recovery. Being eighteen and the youngest, Marc had no recollection of his father ever drinking, but Taylor, who was twenty-three, vividly remembered the pain alcohol had caused their family. For that reason, along with many others, Marc was stunned that Taylor had become an addict.

"What happened with Taylor?" Marc's mother asked as soon as he walked into the living room. His parents were sitting together on the sofa, watching RedZone. Football had always been a staple in their family.

Marc sat down beside her. "He's way worse off than he led you to believe," he began. "He's worse than I even thought."

"What's going on?" his father asked, sitting up straight and staring Marc directly in the eye.

Marc swallowed deeply. "I know you guys want to believe he's just depressed over getting injured and losing his scholarship, but it's so much more than that."

"You and Jordan tried to tell us he was misusing his meds, and I'm sorry we didn't take you more seriously," his father said. "Taylor was good at appearing like he had a handle on everything... until he stopped talking to us."

Marc swallowed deeply. "It's not even that he's misusing his meds. He's moved onto stronger stuff now. He has a supplier in Boston who sells him OxyContin. He's been high every time you've seen him this year."

Marc's mother dropped her jaw, widened her eyes, and turned to his father, who looked skeptical. Marc wasn't surprised; his father had been putting Taylor on a pedestal his entire life.

"But you said on the phone he's going through withdrawal," his father stated and eyed Marc in a confused manner.

Marc locked his eyes on his dad. "Drug companies stopped making OCs as caplets because people were abusing them. They're now made of gel, which can't be crushed up and snorted. Taylor's supplier was somehow able to still get the caplets, but he must have run out because Taylor has none left—"

"—Wait," his father interrupted him. "You mean he's been snorting his pills?"

Marc nodded.

Marc's father appeared to be at a loss for words.

"Why hasn't he come to us for help?" his mother asked.

"He doesn't want you to see him like this," Marc replied. "I think he finally realizes he has a problem, but I don't know if he wants to get sober or get high."

"So, he's just sick all the time?" his mother asked.

Marc was trying to hold back as many details as he could to spare his mother's heart, but he needed his parents to understand the gravity of the situation. "He's trying to rid himself of withdrawal symptoms by doing other drugs."

"What other drugs?" his father asked, looking as though he were about to cry.

"I couldn't wake him up when I got there. He was in a trance. I saw some yellow powder in a vial in his room. I feared the worst, but when he woke up he said he had mixed Xanax and Percocet together so he could sleep."

"I need to get to Boston," his father said and stood up abruptly. "Where's his key?"

"Dad, wait. There's more," Marc said and stood up beside his father. "He deals drugs now. Serious drugs."

Marc's mother burst into tears as his father snatched the key out of his hand, grabbed his own keys off the coffee table, and bolted out the front door.

Marc turned and hugged his mother. "Dad will get him the help he needs," he said as he held her tightly in his arms. "Taylor can beat this."

His mother continued sobbing on his shoulder, and Marc could not remember ever feeling so brokenhearted.

CHAPTER 3

AFTER MARC LEFT HIS apartment, Taylor sat upon his sofa with his head in his hands, trying to fight his nausea. Withdrawal. He could not believe he was going through withdrawal. That meant he was addicted to a drug and had likely been addicted for months. That meant Marc and Jordan had been right. His ex-girlfriend Julie had been right. He had become an addict, something he never thought possible, something he arrogantly assumed he was too strong to ever become.

The shame Taylor felt superseded the humiliation he felt when he lost his chance to play for Notre Dame, when he lost his senior season at Northeastern to a knee injury, and when he forced himself to break up with Julie to protect her from the corruption in his life. Losing all of those important things hurt immensely, but losing his brother Marc's respect gauged his heart.

Fighting the nausea was no longer an option shy of taking Percocet. Taylor knew he would need to take at least four pills to mitigate his withdrawal symptoms, but that would just prolong the inevitable and mean that Taylor accepted the identity of drug abuser.

Slowly rising from his couch, Taylor grabbed ahold of his stomach. Sweat was once again seeping from his forehead, and his muscles were spasming like they did after a grueling practice. He stumbled toward his bedroom. It was time to draw a line in the sand.

CHAPTER 4

M R. DUNKIN ARRIVED AT Taylor's apartment around six o'clock that evening. He banged loudly on the door five or six times, expecting no response and hoping the door was not deadbolted. Taylor's Jeep was in the driveway, as were a couple of other cars. Before Mr. Dunkin could pull Taylor's key out of his pocket, the front door began to swing open.

"Mr. D!" Ryan Blake, Taylor's roommate since his freshman year, exclaimed in surprise. "Is everything okay?"

"I need to speak with my son," Mr. Dunkin said and stepped past Ryan into the house.

"Uh, okay... he's in his room," Ryan called out as Mr. Dunkin proceeded down the hallway towards Taylor's bedroom.

Without knocking, Mr. Dunkin whipped open the bedroom door and slammed it behind him. Taylor's room was empty, but the door to his adjoining bathroom was ajar. The sound of someone vomiting was apparent, and Mr. Dunkin soon found his son bowing before the toilet.

Taylor, turning to see who was in his room, fell over when he saw his father. "Dad!"

"What is wrong with you?" Mr. Dunkin hollered as he grabbed Taylor by his shirt and pulled him to his feet. Taylor immediately looked down and began breathing heavily. Sweat was raining down his sickly pale face. He closed his eyes and rested his head against the wall.

"We are going to the hospital right now!" Mr. Dunkin stated firmly.

"No," Taylor said in an exasperated tone. "I can't." With that, he dropped to the floor and began throwing up again.

Mr. Dunkin stared in disbelief that the scene before him was truly happening. Over the years, Taylor had made him prouder than anyone else in the world. He had broken every quarterback's record in his high school's league and scored high enough on the SAT to satisfy every recruiter. In college, he had been ranked by ESPN as one of the NFL's top prospects. Taylor, even more so than his brothers, was a leader and a fighter. Mr. Dunkin could not believe the weak, sickly human being in front of him was his oldest son.

He stepped out of the bathroom and began looking around Taylor's bedroom for the drugs Marc had mentioned. When he found the prescription bottles, he started inspecting each one. They were prescribed to Taylor, but the labels said they were filled over a year ago. He threw the bottles of Xanax, Klonopin, and Percocet onto Taylor's bed, shut the drawer, and opened the one below it. Upon opening the green box that he found, Mr. Dunkin was stunned. This was his worst nightmare.

He grabbed the prescription bottles off Taylor's bed and threw them inside the box. While Taylor continued throwing up in his bathroom, Mr. Dunkin left the bedroom and walked to the half-bath off the kitchen. He locked the door behind him, and bottle by bottle, bag by bag, vial by vial, he flushed every single substance down the toilet.

A moment later, he returned to Taylor's bedroom and placed the box on his bed. Making his way toward the bathroom, he heard his son crying. A second later, he found him lying in the fetal position on the cold bathroom tile. "You have to go to the hospital," Mr. Dunkin demanded.

"I can't," Taylor replied faintly. "This can't be in my medical history—not if I ever want to play for the NFL. I'm already damaged goods from my injury. This would ruin me."

"Taylor, you can't think about football right now. You need to detox."

"No!" Taylor cried out. "I did this to myself. I'll suffer through it."

Mr. Dunkin was somewhat relieved that Taylor seemed to still care about football and his future. He did not know whether to comfort his son or further reprimand him. Many of the drugs that Mr. Dunkin had flushed down the toilet would have mitigated some of the withdrawal symptoms. The fact that Taylor was allowing himself to go through withdrawal led Mr. Dunkin to believe that he wanted to get sober. He knew that someone could not die from opiate withdrawal, and because he had flushed Taylor's stash, he would not overdose. Mr. Dunkin reasoned that the best thing to do was let his son endure the pain.

"How long have you been sick?" Mr. Dunkin asked.

"Since Friday," Taylor replied and stood up in front of the sink. He splashed water on his face and then slumped back down on the floor. He closed his eyes and rested the back of his head against the wall.

"It won't get much worse than this," Mr. Dunkin said. "You'll feel this way for a few more days and then things will start to ease up. You're sure you want to do it this way?"

Taylor let out a heavy breath and nodded.

"Once you're free of this, you won't need a supplier to get you pills," Mr. Dunkin stated.

Without opening his eyes, Taylor nodded.

"And you *will not* deal drugs."

Taylor shot his blue eyes open and looked at his father as though he had seen a ghost.

"I know you've been doing that to support your habit, but if anything is going to jeopardize your future, it's dealing drugs," Mr. Dunkin said matter-of-factly.

Taylor brought his hands to his face and hung his head in shame. "I'm sorry," he mumbled after a moment. "I'm so sorry."

"I'm going to call your mother and tell her I'm staying the night," Mr. Dunkin said, wondering if Taylor would ask him to leave.

Taylor nodded. "That's great, Dad. Thank you."

CHAPTER 5

THE NEXT MORNING, MR. Dunkin watched as Taylor realized his father had destroyed his stash. A look of terror washed over Taylor's face. "Dad, what did you do?"

"I got rid of the drugs that are destroying your life," Mr. Dunkin replied flatly.

"No!" Taylor exclaimed in disbelief. "I owe my supplier money for those. I sell them. Then he takes his cut."

"What's his cut?"

"I can't believe you did that," Taylor said as he hurled over with nausea. He ran out of his bedroom and into the bathroom to resume dry-heaving.

"Taylor, how much do you owe him?" Mr. Dunkin pressed.

"Thousands."

"I'll write you a check."

"No," Taylor said between hurls.

"I want this person out of your life for good. I'll do whatever it takes to help you break away from this."

Taylor lay back down on the floor. "It's my mess. I'll get him the money. I won't cash your check."

"I'll deposit a few thousand dollars into your bank account this afternoon. You can leave it there or use it to pay your debt. Whatever you think is smart. Money means nothing to me, but you mean everything."

"Dad, I don't deserve that," Taylor said. "I have let our entire family down—our entire *town* down. I let my team down. I have failed in every aspect. I deserve the pain I'm going through right now, and I do not deserve your generosity."

"Didn't you learn anything about grace during all those Al-Anon meetings? You're right. You don't deserve it, but that doesn't matter. It is my choice to extend grace to you. It is what you and your mother did for me many, many years ago."

Taylor let out a heavy breath.

"The hardest person to forgive is yourself, but you have to do it, son," Mr. Dunkin admonished him. "You'll get through this, and you'll find yourself again if you stay clean."

Taylor nodded.

"Why don't you come home with me? I'd feel a lot better if you weren't alone."

"Oh, no, Dad. I couldn't. Mom can't see me like this. I can't hurt her like that."

Although Mr. Dunkin wanted Taylor to return home, he realized his son was right. His wife's already broken heart would shatter into pieces if she saw him in this state. "All right, well, I'll check on you later. Keep your phone on and charged. I want to be able to reach you."

Taylor nodded.

"Please come home as soon as you can," Mr. Dunkin said before turning to leave the room. "We miss you so much."

CHAPTER 6

CATHY KAGELLI STARED ACROSS her biology classroom at his freshly cut, jet-black hair. Even from behind, she could tell that he had spent time arranging each gelled spike on his head. Though he was particular about, well, everything, he still would have been the most beautiful boy at Montgomery Lake High if he had come to school directly after rolling out of bed. She couldn't see the expression on his face, but the familiar laugh that echoed across the room ensured that the smile that had been giving her butterflies for two years was plastered across his face. Every so often, whether in the computer hall, science lab, or cafeteria, she would feel his blue eyes resting upon her. Any glance in his direction always resulted in him turning immediately away, as though he were fearful of any connection being made.

Cathy's cell phone vibrated on her lap, pulling her attention away from her ex-boyfriend, Jason Davids. A text had come through from Marc Dunkin—the senior whom she had been "talking to" since December. His text read: *What's up for tonight? Want to go to Luke's game?* She glanced again at the back of Jason's head and traced her eyes down his neck. It wasn't long before she was staring at his arm, picturing the toned bicep beneath his shirt. At that point, she would have given anything to feel his arms around her, just one more time.

Sounds good, she typed into her phone. As she sent the text to Marc, she wondered if Jason would be at his brother's game. After all, Luke had recently been promoted to captain, which was quite an honor for a junior. Without waiting for Marc's response, she put her phone inside her pocketbook.

"Okay, all the stations are set up," Cathy's biology teacher announced. "You know the drill: last names that begin with A through H start on the left, I through P in the middle, and everyone else on the right. Move clockwise around the room."

Cathy watched Jason jump off his stool and hustle toward the back-left corner of the lab. He was the first to reach the observation station, followed by his best friend Chris Dunkin.

"You know I have no patience," Jason said loudly to Chris. "Let's get this done!" He laughed and stepped toward a microscope.

CHAPTER 7

A HALF HOUR LATER, CATHY exited her science class, scanning the sea of freshmen flooding the hallway. She was looking for the piercing green eyes that could best read her own. A moment later, she felt someone gently tap her arm. "I was just looking for you," she said to her best friend Lisa Ankerman as she glanced over her shoulder.

Lisa's facial expression fell. "You just came from bio, huh?"

Cathy nodded.

Lisa squinted and appeared to be contemplating a response. Her eyes filled with concern. "I hate seeing you so affected by him."

"I try not to be. I just...I don't know who I am apart from him."

"Yes, you do," Lisa said with certainty. "I liked you when I met you because you knew exactly who you were."

"Yeah, in seventh grade!" Cathy exclaimed. "That was before I lost myself in Jason."

"What do you have next period? Study?"

Cathy nodded.

"All right. I'll see if Mr. B will give me a pass to the library. I'll text you if I can make it."

"How are you going to get out of English?"

Lisa smiled. "He's the varsity basketball coach, and I'm a varsity cheerleader. We connect."

Cathy laughed. "More like he's only twenty-three, and you're the prettiest girl in our grade!"

CHAPTER 8

***

One Day later

To: Cathy
From: Jason
3/29/18

So much has happened over the last few months. It is hard to even know where to begin this note. When this year started, I never thought we would go a full day without speaking, let alone four months. This letter is so hard to write because I have so many regrets. I never stopped loving you. Even in my deepest anger, even when I sent all your calls to voicemail, you were still the love of my life. I needed to distance myself from our lifestyle to sober up, but I never wanted to distance myself from you.

When I see you in school, the vacant look in your eye makes me so sad. I'm not sure what drug is stealing away bits of your soul these days, but everything I hear about Luke is horrifying. I'm sorry that my quest to find myself caused you pain. Drugs stole my identity, and now, they are stealing yours. But I found out that the person I used to be still existed inside of me. I know the girl I fell in love with is still somewhere inside of you. You left an amazing life behind you—and everyone in it misses you more than you know.

Two years ago, I fell in love with a witty, fun-loving, auburn-haired girl who was full of good morals and faith that I didn't understand. I pulled you away from all of that. I introduced you to the worst things in your life, and it bothers me every day.

I know you are with Marc, and I know he is a great guy. I don't want to cause any problems between you two by asking to come back into your life. I just want to offer my support and apologize for being such a bad influence on you.

Two years ago, I fell in love with a beautiful person. I believe she still exists, somewhere, beneath it all. And in my heart, I carry the hope that she still loves me, too.

Cathy stood in silence at her locker, reading her ex-boyfriend's letter. She took a deep breath and tried to understand the emotions overcoming her body. He had not spoken to her since November. Every day, he would pass by her in the halls and look past her, as though she were a stranger, as though they had never been in love.

She was staring at her name written in Jason's neat handwriting when she felt a warm hand upon her back. Folding the letter in half, she glanced over her shoulder to see Marc and Luke standing beside her. They were the best-looking upperclassmen at MLH, but for once she didn't want their attention; she wanted to be alone with her thoughts.

"Hey," she greeted them, attempting to sound at ease.

"Do you want to get out of here?" Luke whispered and nodded toward the exit.

Cathy lowered her eyebrows and glanced skeptically from Luke to Marc. It was not like Marc to skip class. Although seniors could freely sign themselves in and out of school, Marc rarely took advantage of it. "Where are you going?" she asked.

"Boston," Luke stated flatly.

"Now?" Cathy questioned him and slid Jason's letter into her pocket.

"No more questions," Marc said in a playful tone. "Let's go, beautiful," he added and threw his muscular arm around her shoulders.

CHAPTER 9

L EAVING SCHOOL WAS NOT an easy feat, but thankfully Cathy's friends knew about all the quirks in the system. That year, the athletic department had chosen to spend its funds on new uniforms instead of upgrading its security system, which rendered the cameras incompatible with the rest of the school's equipment. This created the perfect escape route for the few athletes who knew about the loophole. Since Marc could not be seen leaving the senior parking lot with a freshman and a junior, he had to pick up Cathy and Luke outside of the gym.

"So, what's going on in Boston?" Cathy questioned Luke while they waited outside in the cold for Marc.

"Marc has a meeting with the coaches at BC," Luke replied, "so I offered to take the ride with him."

"That's where we're going?"

Luke laughed. "Well, we are dropping him off at BC," he said with a smirk, "and then going on an adventure."

"You're not going to say more than that, are you?" Cathy gathered, knowing that Luke enjoyed building suspense.

"Not until we drop off your boyfriend."

"He's not my boyfriend," Cathy said and rolled her eyes. "Missy couldn't come?" she asked, referring to Luke's girlfriend.

Luke shook his head. "No. She's still in trouble with her parents for getting kicked off cheer. She hasn't skipped school since. I still feel like a jerk for getting her in trouble," he admitted. "Going to that rave was my idea. Did you know Jay almost came with us?"

At the sound of Jason's name, Cathy's heart began to pound. "No," she replied flatly.

"Yeah, I invited him, but he flipped out and made me drive him to school."

That must have been when he was trying to sober up. "I'm all set with talking about your brother," she stated firmly, spotting Marc's red truck heading toward them.

"That's fair," Luke remarked and draped his arm around Cathy's shoulders. "Let's get out of here."

When Cathy climbed into the backseat of Marc's truck, she hoped whatever Luke had planned would keep Jason off her mind.

"So, Cathy, I have a meeting at BC about my commitment for next year," Marc said as they drove away from the school. "The meeting goes 'til four, so Luke is going to entertain you until it's time to pick me up," he continued. "Do you need to be home at a certain time?"

"I'll call my mom after school and tell her that I'm going with Luke to pick you up at BC," Cathy said. "She'll probably say I can hang out until my curfew. Since there's no school tomorrow, I should be good if I'm home by eleven."

"That works," Marc said in his usual, agreeable tone. "If our friends meet us in Boston, Luke can stay with them, and I'll take you home."

"There's a reason my parents like you so much," Cathy said with a smile.

"Just don't get into too much trouble when you leave BC," Marc joked and playfully hit Luke in the arm. "Go sightseeing or something; have lunch on Newbury Street; visit the Bruins Pro Shop; go skate on the frog pond— just make sure you're back to campus before four o'clock."

"No problem, dude," Luke assured him. "We'll find something to do."

Cathy assumed Luke already had a plethora of ideas running through his mind. After dating his younger brother for almost two years, she knew Luke well. Because of Luke and Marc's differing opinions about drugs, she found it odd that they were best friends but presumed Marc did not know the half of what Luke did behind closed doors. She felt bad that Marc was likely in the dark, but telling him about Luke's drug use would only expose her own dark past.

CHAPTER 10

"OKAY, CK—YOU READY FOR some fun?" Luke asked a half hour later as he and Cathy sat in Marc's truck, watching him walk across BC's campus.

"What do you have in mind?" Cathy questioned him suspiciously. "Do you really know your way around Boston well enough to get back here in a few hours?"

Luke nodded. "Marc has a GPS. We'll be fine. You've got to trust me." The way Luke turned and smiled at her reminded her so much of Jason that her heart fluttered. Although Jason looked more like his oldest brother Matt, he and Luke both had their father's handsome smile.

"How can I not trust that smile?" Cathy remarked. She watched as Luke typed a South Boston address into the GPS. From what Cathy knew of Boston, Southie seemed like a rather far drive from Chestnut Hill.

"We're going to visit Taylor," Luke announced once they turned out of BC's campus.

A lump formed in Cathy's throat. "Does Marc know?"

"No," Luke replied, keeping his hazel eyes on the road. "They haven't talked in a while."

"I *know*," Cathy stated emphatically, hoping her tone made it clear she was uncomfortable with the idea.

"It's gonna be fine."

"They haven't talked in months."

"Marc doesn't need to know."

"Taylor devastated their family!" Cathy exclaimed in complete awe that Luke associated with Marc's wayward brother.

"Cathy, trust me. I talk to Taylor a lot. I told him I would stop by."

Cathy darted her green eyes at him. "Is he your supplier?" she asked, realizing drugs were likely the reason Luke was in touch with Taylor.

"T hooks me up," Luke replied, still peering at the road. "He has connections I could never have as a junior at MLH."

"Oh my God," Cathy said in disbelief. "*Marc's brother* supplies you with drugs to sell in Montgomery? So, all the pills I've taken have come from *him*?"

"Why do you sound pissed?" Luke asked, quickly glancing over at her.

Cathy widened her eyes and let out a heavy breath. "So, Taylor's the one who got Chris all messed up? Did he know who you were giving drugs to?"

"Where do you think I get the prescription stuff from?" Luke questioned her. "Do you really think I steal it from my parents or buy it off someone in Montgomery?"

"Sadly, I never gave it any thought," Cathy admitted.

Marc had talked to her about Taylor *a lot*. He was, after all, a living legend in their town: "the best athlete to ever step foot in Montgomery." Marc recapped hours of phone conversations spent trying to help Taylor see he could still have a future in football if he sobered up. Marc said that drugs were stealing his brother's will. It frightened Cathy that painkillers could change someone's personality so drastically.

"Don't be pissed at me," Luke stated defensively while steering Marc's truck toward the Mass Pike.

Cathy suddenly felt sick to her stomach. "How does Marc not know? He would be so upset if he knew Taylor got you into drugs."

"Believe me when I say Marc isn't naïve," Luke stated matter-of-factly. "He probably knows a lot more than you think. I don't tell anyone I get my stuff from Taylor."

"Well, he'll see Taylor's address in his GPS," Cathy said, motioning toward the device.

"He doesn't know Taylor's address. The last time they talked, Taylor lived in JP. As long as we go to some restaurant on Broadway, he will just assume that was its address."

"I see you have it all figured out."

"To play it safe, we shouldn't tell Taylor you're going out with Marc."

"We're not official,'" Cathy corrected him. "And doesn't it make you sad to see Taylor like this? I mean, you've known him your whole life. You must have looked up to him. To see him throw all his talent away and turn into a drug addict—doesn't that upset you?"

"I think it's sad his injury left him hung up on pills that made him too tired to go to class and led to him being ineligible to play football. I feel bad for him."

"You make it sound like he didn't crush up the pills to get high!" Cathy cried. "Blowing OC-80s is different from taking painkillers orally. Not to mention, he could have taken a medical leave of absence from school and only been behind by one trimester. He did this to himself."

"Oh my God! You sound like Marc!" Luke exclaimed and started laughing. "CK! What's happened to you?"

"Marc explained *everything* to me about Taylor," Cathy stated. "Painkillers turned him into an addict, which caused him to fail out of his major and lose his scholarship."

"Sounds like Marc talks about T a lot," Luke commented, sounding genuinely surprised. "I'm sorry. I had no idea you knew that much about him. You don't have to come inside with me if it'll make you feel uncomfortable."

If I wait in the truck, then I won't get to see what Taylor looks like now. "If I wait in the truck, you'll have to keep it running because it's so cold out. I don't want to waste Marc's gas."

"I can just refill the tank," Luke offered in a light-hearted manner. "It's totally up to you. We don't have to stay long. I do have other things in mind for today."

"According to the GPS, we'll be there in twenty minutes," Cathy said and leaned her head against the window. "I'll figure it out."

CHAPTER 11

DETECTIVE ADAM ST. JAMES of the Boston Police Department peered at the photographs, diagrams, and timelines surrounding him and the task force he led. He, along with five other detectives, had been building a case against a local organized crime ring for the last six months. They were huddled in a small room inside the BPD Headquarters.

Their main focus had been placed upon Donald Bilotti, a forty-four-year-old Caucasian drug dealer who had been residing in Boston's Mission Hill neighborhood for the last three years. Living in an area comprised mainly of college kids and low-income housing had proven to be very beneficial for Mr. Bilotti. However, after a sharp rise in overdoses were reported on college campuses nearby, Detective St. James and his team had been tasked with taking down the Bilotti crime ring.

Fourteen pictures of individuals who were presumed to work for Donny Bilotti lay on the table before the detectives. The people in the photographs ranged in age from sixteen to sixty-three—all white, living in different Boston neighborhoods.

"He's our weak link," Adam said as he pointed to a picture of a blonde-haired, blue-eyed, twenty-three-year-old. "Taylor Dunkin moved across the city, changed his number, and has not had any visitors of interest at his new apartment. He wants out."

"But he wants to stay alive," Detective Susan Winters commented, "so he isn't going to rat on his boss unless he has no other choice."

"Donny Bilotti ran everything from molly to heroin through Mr. Dunkin for the last year, making hundreds of thousands of dollars," Adam explained. "As the star of Northeastern's football team, Taylor was invited to every party on that campus. He was Bilotti's MVP. There is no way in hell Donny let him off scot-free. Taylor would be better off dead to him than out of the game, and Donny's bosses tie up their loose ends. As clean as Taylor looks to us from the outside, he must still be pushing if he's still alive."

"How does a kid with a full scholarship to college, from a good Catholic family, with a bright athletic future get mixed up with Donald Bilotti?" Detective Marty O'Reilly asked and shook his head.

Adam pulled a picture out of a folder from a football game a year-and-a-half prior. "A sports injury led to a couple of knee surgeries and an opiate addiction. We have evidence that suggests Mr. Dunkin got pulled into the ring by another Northeastern student, Robert Anuzelli."

"It's sad, but the number of overdoses that have occurred on college campuses because of Mr. Bilotti's and Mr. Dunkin's business arrangement is sadder," Detective Winters stated matter-of-factly.

"We know Taylor still has Bilotti's drugs in his possession," Adam asserted. "If we were to raid his place right now, we could take him down, but he's not going to rat on his boss. If he did, Bilotti's men would go after his family, and he knows that. Taylor's youngest brother Marc will be attending BC next year. His other brother Jordan is across the country playing football for Notre Dame, but he's still not out of Bilotti's reach. This kid has no shot at getting out of this alive without cooperating with us."

"His family is crucial to this," Detective Winters stressed. "Prior to his injury, Taylor was very close with them. He's going to do whatever he needs to do to protect them, whether that means continuing to deal drugs or becoming an informant."

"So, if we can get him to wear a wire and pick up a batch of drugs from Bilotti's stash house, we'll have the evidence we need to seize the property," Adam stated. "We would get a warrant ahead of time, based off of Dunkin's sealed testimony, so the deal caught on record would be admissible."

"Taylor would have to do time or else Bilotti would know he was the rat," Detective James Roth reasoned.

"He's not going to want to do time," Detective O'Reilly said and shook his head. "The kid was an NFL top prospect. If he's trying to get out of the game, he's likely sober, wanting to get back on the field."

"If we give him immunity, then Bilotti will know he's the snitch," Detective Winters remarked and turned towards Adam. "We can't put the entire Dunkin family into witness protection. Jordan Dunkin is a nationally recognized college football player."

"So, we wait until there's a meeting with multiple dealers at Bilotti's place," Adam proposed. "We don't prosecute anyone but Donny. He'll never know who wore the wire. We'll get our guy. None of his dealers are big names. They're not connected to the people Bilotti's connected to. Once we have Bilotti, we can see if he'll accept a plea bargain in exchange for evidence against his supplier."

"That would be the win of the decade for this department," Detective O'Reilly commented and raised his eyebrows.

"So, that's it?" Detective Winters asked. "We put all our hopes in this kid?" She picked up Taylor's picture and then glanced at the men surrounding her.

Adam nodded. "He'll do whatever he needs to do to get out of this. He's our guy. We just have to rope him in inconspicuously. Roth, you're going to head over to BC. Lose the suit; dress like a professor. This kid," Adam said and held up a picture, "Taylor's brother Marc has a meeting with the football coaches this afternoon. You will interrupt the meeting, clear the room, and privately give Marc this burner phone with my number in it." Adam slid a black flip-phone toward Detective Roth. "Tell him we know Taylor wants out of the game, and we want to help him get out alive. We can't go near Taylor without raising suspicion, but Bilotti doesn't have men watching Marc. Marc will cooperate. He knows his brother is in deep."

Detective Roth nodded and stood up from the table. "What do you want me to say to the coaches?"

"I've informed them that Marc is of great importance to us on a confidential case," Adam replied. "They are planning to offer him a starting spot next year, so they need him safe just as much as we do."

Detective Roth nodded. "Back to my roots, I go," he said before walking out the door.

CHAPTER 12

BACK IN MONTGOMERY, JASON Davids sat at his usual lunch table, thinking about the letter he had written to Cathy. She normally ate lunch at the table next to his with Lisa—if she didn't sit with Marc—but she had not shown her pretty face inside the cafeteria yet. Jason peered across the room to his oldest brother Matt's table to see if Marc was there. He saw a bunch of familiar faces but not Marc.

"What's up, Jay?" Chris Dunkin asked, breaking through Jason's contemplation. "You're way too quiet."

Jason glanced at his friends sitting around him: Chris Dunkin, Cathy's identical twin sister Chantal, Andy Rosetti, Jon Anderson, Alyssa Kelly, Bryan Sartelli, and Courtney Angeletti. He trusted them all. "I slipped a letter into Cathy's locker this morning," he admitted. "She's been on my mind a lot lately, so I decided to reach out."

"Wow," Chantal said and widened her bright green eyes.

Chris raised his eyebrows and sent Jason a hard-to-read look.

"I don't think she's in a good place," Jason added.

"She's going out with Marc," Chris said, sounding a bit defensive of his cousin. "He's a good influence on everyone. What are you trying to accomplish?"

Jason scratched his ear and looked away. "I don't know. It just felt like the right thing to do. I'm not trying to break them up. I just want her to know I'm sorry for the way things ended between us."

"I think she's doing better than she was a few months ago," Chris commented. "Marc told me she made some changes at his request."

Jason took a deep breath. "I know her, and I just know in my gut that something's not right. It's an aura she gives off, a look in her eye. I can't really describe it, but I can't shake the feeling that she's in a bad place. This time, it might not even be with drugs. It could be emotional or mental—I don't know. Chantal, you must get a sense of her when you see her at home."

Chantal shrugged. "We don't talk."

"Lisa's worried," Jason said, "and that concerns me because she has good intuition. Who knows if anything will come of my letter? Cathy could just tear it up. I just wanted to reach out to see if there's anything I could do to help."

Chantal stared at Jason with an endearing smile, which told him she was pleased he had reached out to her twin.

"Jay, don't entangle yourself with Cathy again," Bryan spoke up. "She's not the girl we used to love. That girl's been gone for a while. She messes with your head."

Jason felt that Bryan knew better than anyone how hard his and Cathy's breakup had been on him. Bryan also knew how much Cathy meant to Jason and how difficult it had been for him to cut ties with her to get sober. Jason knew Bryan's words were spoken from a place of care; however, he was underestimating how much stronger Jason had grown in his sobriety. "I'm not going to relapse," he stated assuredly.

"I don't think you are," Bryan responded matter-of-factly, "but I've seen the power she has over you—we all have."

Jason rolled his eyes. "She is the way she is because of me. I ruined her. She had the best intentions when we met. I got her into stuff last year that just... destroyed her. I am to blame for the hot mess that is now Cathaleen Kagelli."

Bryan sighed.

He knows I'm right, Jason thought.

Chris let out a heavy breath.

He knows it, too.

"Like, what, Jay?" Chantal asked and locked her troubled green eyes on him.

Jason dropped his eyes to his hands. He knew Chantal would become distraught if she found out the extent of her twin's drug use. As far as he knew, Chantal was only aware of Cathy smoking pot. Chris knew everything; Bryan and Alyssa knew some things; Courtney, Jon, and Andy knew hardly anything. "I can't get into it here," he replied quietly. "We can talk later."

Chantal lowered her eyebrows with concern and then nodded.

CHAPTER 13

CATHY STOOD BESIDE LUKE at Taylor's door with a pounding heart.

"Hey, Luke! What's up, man?" Taylor greeted him warmly as he whipped open his door. He slapped hands with Luke in a very "bro" way and then stepped aside to let them into his apartment. His shirt was off, revealing his six-pack abs and V-shaped torso.

You still look like an athlete, Cathy thought as she looked him up and down. *You're as hot as ever.*

"T, this is Cathy," Luke said, motioning toward her. "You might remember her. She dated Jay-dawg for a couple of years."

"Oh, yeah. Hey, Cathy. Good to see you," Taylor said and smiled warmly.

"You, too," Cathy replied while studying his appearance.

Taylor's blonde hair was neatly styled, his pants were wrinkleless, his face was clean-shaven, and his pupils were normal-sized.

I would never think you were a drug addict if I passed you on the street, Cathy thought as she followed Taylor through a tidy kitchen to a finely decorated living room. NHL Network was on the TV, and a stack of *Sports Illustrated* magazines were on the coffee table.

"So, what brings you into Boston today?" Taylor asked as he sat down in a beige leather recliner. "No school?"

"No school for us," Luke replied as he sat down on the couch with Cathy. "A few of our friends are meeting us in town later. There's no school tomorrow because of Good Friday."

"Oh, right," Taylor replied and lowered the TV. "Do you guys want anything to eat or drink?"

"I'm all set," Luke said. "We'll grab lunch after we leave."

"Thanks anyway," Cathy replied, finding herself at ease around Taylor. It was strange to see him so calm. The only time she had ever spent with him was during parties, when he had always been the center of attention. She had never seen him sober—if he was.

"How's Marc?" Taylor asked and locked his blue eyes on Luke.

"He's great," Luke replied. "He's all ready for BC next year. He's good."

"Good," Taylor said. "He'll do well."

Cathy wondered if it bothered Taylor to hear that Marc, like his other brother Jordan, would be playing college ball. Marc told Cathy that five years prior, multiple colleges with ranked Division I football teams had offered Taylor athletic scholarships. However, after a supposed "senior-prank-gone-wrong" led to Taylor's arrest, the prestigious university he signed with rescinded its offer. By then, the SEC and ACC schools that had tried to recruit him had already signed other quarterbacks, so Taylor was left with minimal options. Therefore, he enrolled as a business major at Northeastern University.

"How do you like living in Southie?" Luke asked. "A lot better than JP?"

"It's a great area," Taylor replied. "There are a lot of kids my age and a lot of cool bars and restaurants. I'm glad I made the move. I needed a change."

"I'll probably come to college in Boston," Luke stated. "The city draws me in."

"Yeah, you're up here enough," Taylor laughed. He reached for a small wooden box on the table and pulled out a dab pen, likely filled with marijuana oil. "Do you want to hit this?"

Cathy widened her eyes. *Of course, I do*, she thought, *but I can't, or your brother will ostracize me.* She darted her eyes at Luke.

"Weed?" Luke asked.

Taylor nodded.

"I'm not a fan," Luke replied, "but I'll test out some other product if you've got anything."

"What are you looking for?" Taylor asked and set the vaporizer back inside its box.

"I'm going to a club later, so something speedy," Luke explained. "Also a few kids in my grade were asking if I could get them Xanax."

"Let me see what I have left," Taylor said and stood up. Cathy watched his muscles move as he walked out of the room.

"Are you okay being here?" Luke questioned Cathy once Taylor left the room.

"It's a little awkward," Cathy whispered. "He doesn't expect me to try stuff, right?"

Luke shrugged. "You don't have to try anything, whether he thinks you will or not. Just ask to go to the bathroom if things get uncomfortable or ask me for a cigarette and go outside."

"Ew! I don't smoke!" Cathy cried defensively.

"Oh, right. The cigarettes Missy bought were for 'your friends.'"

"They were," Cathy stated adamantly. "Why do you have cigarettes? You don't smoke."

"It's a social thing," Luke replied carelessly.

"Luke!" Cathy cried angrily and slapped his arm. "Gross!" She didn't know what Taylor was going to offer them, but she was feeling a bit overwhelmed. Truthfully, the idea of getting high sounded appealing because she wanted to suppress her feelings about Jason.

A minute later, Taylor came back into the room with a green box. He put it down on the table and pulled out a small bag of capsules. "Those are the best around," he said as he tossed the bag at Luke. "Don't take a whole capsule at once and don't take any of it until right before you go into the club. Otherwise, you'll look too messed up to get in."

"How many are in here?" Luke asked as he sifted through the bag of molly.

"About two dozen. You can sell them to your friends for fifteen. They're potent, so that's a good deal," Taylor replied. "I still have Adderall if you think anyone wants it."

"I think they'll all want these," Luke said. "I know I do."

Cathy couldn't help but wonder who else was planning to roll that night. She knew Marc certainly wasn't.

"Do you have any Xanax, Percocet, Vicodin, or Klonopin?" Luke asked. "There's a big market for those at my school."

"Sorry, I'm clean out of benzos and painkillers," Taylor replied immediately.

Cathy assumed Taylor had probably snorted all the painkillers. Marc was afraid he had turned to heroin, but Taylor certainly didn't look like a heroin addict. He had no track marks up his arms, and he hadn't lost any weight. Although heroin was the natural progression for someone who had been snorting painkillers for a while, Cathy knew that usually happened when addicts ran out of money or product. By the looks of Taylor's lavishly furnished condo and large supply of drugs, it did not seem like he was hurting for either.

"I'll take some coke if you have it," Luke said. "I have some friends who will do it with me. Do you have any of the stuff from a few months ago?"

Taylor pulled a small bag of white powder out from his box and poured some of it onto the table. "Same stuff. You can try it if you want."

Cathy's heart pounded as Luke took a dollar bill out of his wallet and rolled it up. She widened her eyes as he leaned forward and blew the thin line set before him. She had never actually seen anyone do coke. Luke didn't hesitate at all, which made her think he did it more often than she had thought. Cathy felt her anxiety rising. "Can I use your bathroom?" she asked, struggling to find her voice.

"Sure. It's right off the kitchen," Taylor replied nonchalantly. "How is it?" he questioned Luke as Cathy began walking out of the room.

"Great," Luke replied.

Cathy hoped they would finish their drug exchange while she was out of the room—although, she was curious to find out what Taylor had been up to lately. To her, he seemed perfectly sober, but she knew something terrible must have happened for Marc to cut ties with him a few months prior.

To Cathy's dismay, the green box was still open on the coffee table when she returned from the bathroom. Luke had the bag of capsules and a small bag of coke in front of him. "While you were gone, T found some Xanax," he said as Cathy sat down beside him. "You seem anxious. Why don't you take one?"

Cathy let out a heavy breath. Luke and Taylor were both staring at her expectantly. She knew they were just trying to help, but their idea of "help" was far different from Marc's... and Marc would lose all respect for her if she took a pill she wasn't prescribed, right? And that would just put more space between Jason and her, right? So, nothing good would come from taking Xanax, right? Cathy blinked for the first time in what felt like five minutes. Her heart was pounding, her palms were beginning to sweat, and she feared she was on the verge of a full-fledged anxiety attack, which just exacerbated everything.

"You know what? Coke always makes me want to smoke," Luke announced suddenly and jumped up from the couch. "T, can I go out on your balcony? Cathy, do you want to come?"

Cathy nodded intently, wondering if he was trying to give her an out or if he actually wanted a cigarette. Luke was so preppy; she couldn't picture him smoking anything.

"Sure," Taylor replied and pointed toward the sliding glass door on the wall opposite them. "Just close it tight behind you."

"Let's go," Luke said to Cathy as he put on his gray peacoat and nodded toward the door.

When they stepped outside, the frigid air slapped Cathy across the face and jolted her attention away from her thoughts. Luke pulled the door shut behind them and turned immediately toward her. On his face was the most serious expression Cathy had ever seen him wear.

"Are you okay?" he asked as he placed his hands on her shoulders and stared directly into her eyes.

She stared back at him, aware that she looked like a deer in headlights. "No," she stated once she found her voice.

"What can I do to make this better?" Luke asked, holding his gaze on her.

"Maybe I should just take a bar of Xanax," Cathy said and looked away from him. "Being here is giving me anxiety about Marc. I can't think straight."

"Is something else bothering you?" Luke asked, removing his hands from her shoulders. "You've seemed off all day."

Cathy looked up into Luke's beautiful hazel eyes. She didn't want to mention Jason in fear he would tell Jason or Marc. She had to keep *that* to herself, but Luke knew her well enough to know something was on her mind. "I just miss smoking weed," she blurted out after a few seconds of thought. "I hate that when my mind races and my heart palpitates I can't get high to calm down. I hate that I get anxiety and have no way to deal with it anymore. I'm driving myself crazy with my crystal-clear, overactive mind."

Luke pulled an unopened pack of cigarettes out of his jacket pocket and began unwrapping it. "Well, there are plenty of things here that could help you with that, and you know I would never tell Marc. I wouldn't have offered Xanax to you unless I thought you needed it. I was trying to help."

Cathy brought her hands to her head and took a deep breath. "I know."

"I can't get through a cigarette right now," Luke said before lighting one. "You're going to have to help me with this. I'm way too sober."

"I'm completely sober!" Cathy protested.

"Well, Taylor can see us out here, so it has to look like I came outside to smoke."

"I'm not smoking," Cathy stated flatly.

"It could help your anxiety."

"It doesn't."

"Well, what about going for counseling?" Luke asked, staring at her thoughtfully.

Cathy shook her head. "My parents would make me see a counselor at their church. I can't do that. I had a bad experience there. It would just compound the problem."

"If they knew how torn up you are, I bet they'd let you see anyone you wanted."

"You don't know my parents. They think you can live your entire life inside a church. They wouldn't want me to get advice from someone who doesn't share our beliefs."

"That sounds smothering."

Cathy nodded. "It is."

"Jason's been going to your church with Chris lately," Luke said nonchalantly. "He doesn't talk to me about it, but I can see he's into it. I don't know why I'm surprised. When he was a kid, he wanted to be a priest."

"He did?" Cathy asked, cocking her head to the side.

"Yeah, until I told him a bunch of priests raped little boys," Luke replied and shook his head with disgust.

Cathy widened her eyes. "The pastors at my church are all married with kids of their own," she said. "My issue was never with my pastors. They're all nice."

"Good!" Luke exclaimed. "My brother's almost as good-looking as me."

Cathy rolled her eyes. "Stop bringing up Jay!"

Luke smirked. "Well, what about talking to Marc?" he suggested and tossed his hardly smoked cigarette over the balcony and into the snow. "He's a supportive and caring guy."

Cathy shook her head. "I'm embarrassed that *we* are even talking about this right now, and you're practically family. I hate talking about myself."

"Yeah, but it's helpful, right? You seem calmer," Luke said and raised his eyebrows.

Cathy sighed. "I feel a little better, but that's probably because we're away from Taylor."

"We can leave."

"Good. I might take that Xanax, though," Cathy said.

"Good!" Luke exclaimed. "Don't worry. I won't tell Jason."

"You mean Marc," Cathy corrected him.

"No, I mean Jay," Luke retorted with a glimmer in his eye.

Cathy eyed Luke precariously. "Stop bringing him up!" she protested.

Luke smirked. "I have my reasons."

Cathy peered at him curiously.

"Anyway..."

"Your reasons?"

"Let's go back inside," Luke said and draped his arm around Cathy. "It's freezing out here!"

"Just give me another minute," Cathy said while shivering, "and tell me why you keep bringing up Jay."

Luke cocked his head to the side and smiled. "Really? You need me to spell it out for you?"

Cathy squinted in confusion and stared at him expectantly.

Luke laughed. "You'll figure it out in due time."

Cathy rolled her eyes. She assumed Luke was trying to figure out if she was truly into Marc or still hung up on Jason. Whether he was looking out for his best friend or for his brother, Cathy could not tell. She knew, however, that she could not allow Luke a glimpse at her feelings until she sorted them out herself. Her journey with Jason had begun two years ago, when she had been a completely different person—evidently one who Jason still loved.

CHAPTER 14

AFTER THE LAST BELL of the day, Jason ventured to Chantal's locker.
"Hey," Chantal greeted him with a small smile as she dropped her maroon bookbag to the floor. "Do you want to talk before I head to practice?"

"If you're up for it," Jason replied, trying to calm his nerves.

"I have about twenty minutes," she said as she shut her locker.

"Let's see how far we get, and I can call you later if I need to—but we can't talk here. Let's find a quiet spot near the gym."

"Okay," Chantal agreed.

As Jason walked with Chantal toward the gym, he debated with himself over how much of Cathy's past to divulge. Chantal was a kind-hearted person, who typically saw the best in everyone. At the beginning of eighth grade, Chantal cut Cathy out of her life for reasons Cathy never understood. The tarnished relationship between the twins had always perplexed Jason.

Once they reached the gym, Jason led Chantal over to the bright-blue bleachers against the back wall, far away from any athletes.

"I know a lot has happened this year," he began after sitting down beside Chantal, "but more has been going on with your sister than you realize."

"I know something is wrong with her," Chantal admitted, "but she doesn't confide in me anymore."

"See, that's part of the problem," Jason said and took a deep breath.

"That she doesn't open up to people?"

Jason shook his head. "No. The feud between the two of you drove her to do things that she normally would never have done. She lost herself in the process, and I am largely to blame for that."

"You are not to blame for Cathy's insanity," Chantal insisted. "No one blames you, not even my parents."

"But they should," Jason stated. "Cathy always cared a lot about other people—too much—and it caused her a significant amount of pain. When we were together, I taught her ways to protect herself. I thought I was helping her, but I was actually ruining her. Once I realized, it was too late. The girl I had fallen in love with was gone. I tried for months to get her back, but I was grasping at straws.

"I've retraced the last two years over and over again, trying to understand how everything fell apart. I keep coming back to a decision that Lisa and I talked Cathy into. We convinced her that she was protecting you—and we thought we were, too—but what we did tore her up inside."

Chantal lowered her eyebrows in a perplexed manner. "What did you guys do to me?!"

CHAPTER 15

***

Two Years Prior - March 2016

CATHY KNEELED AT THE edge of her bed and bowed her head in prayer. *Dear God, I don't understand why my best is never good enough. I follow your rules; I honor my parents; I put my siblings first; yet I'm always the third wheel, the awkward one out, the girl who doesn't know her place. Please put a friend in my life who will accept me as I am. I am so lonely, every day. In Jesus name, Amen.*

Standing up from her bed, she glanced out the window, wondering when the sun would melt away the snow. Although she enjoyed skiing, she missed being able to kick a soccer ball around in her backyard. Sports were her favorite outlet for stress because they helped her focus on the present moment.

Gifted with a strong, analytical mind, Cathy always felt obligated to put her brainpower to use in productive ways. When she was not intently focused on a task, conversation, or challenge, she tended to over-analyze her shortcomings. She was beginning to think her thought pattern might be somewhat unhealthy. However, confessing such a thing to anyone would make her feel like even more of an outcast, which would only compound the problem.

"Cathy!" Chantal's ever-perky voice cried out from behind Cathy's closed bedroom door. "Are you up?"

Before Cathy could respond, Chantal entered the room, looking as though she had just rolled out of bed.

"What's up?" Cathy asked, perceiving the excited look in her twin sister's eyes.

"Jon kissed me last night!" Chantal exclaimed. "Our first kiss! After youth group, we went to his friend Chris's house—the one who Lisa Ankerman is dating. Before Mom picked us up, Jon and I were alone for a few minutes because Chris and Lisa went upstairs. He told me that he loved me, and then he leaned in and kissed me."

I wonder what Chris and Lisa were doing upstairs, Cathy thought immediately. "So, wait, like a *real* kiss or just a kiss on the lips?" she asked.

"What's the difference?"

"Did he stick his tongue down your throat?" Cathy asked, trying not to laugh at her sister's naiveté.

"Ewe, no!" Chantal shrieked. "Gross."

Cathy shook her head and rolled her eyes. "Well, watch out because that will be next."

"Jon's a gentleman," Chantal retorted.

"Unlike Chris, evidently," Cathy remarked, "if he took Lisa upstairs."

"Ever since I stopped talking to Andy, Lisa is not that friendly to me," Chantal said. "I thought they went upstairs to get away from me. I don't think Lisa likes me and Jon together."

"She's just territorial of her best friend," Cathy commented. "You know Andy is still hung up on you. I'm sure it bothers her to see him that way. Lisa's kind of an icicle, anyway. I don't know Chris, but I think it's remarkable that he got her to go out with him."

"I wish Chris would come to youth group so you could meet him," Chantal said. "I think you guys are a lot alike. That's probably why Lisa likes both of you."

"You think Lisa likes me?" Cathy asked. "She has barely said a word to me since we stopped eating lunch with her and Andy. I think her allegiance to Andy pretty much dashed any hopes of a budding friendship between her, you, and me."

Chantal shrugged. "She asked for you last night."

"Really?"

Chantal nodded.

"Hmm, maybe I should hang out with you guys sometime," Cathy said. "I would just feel weird if it was me and all couples."

"Jon has single friends! Alyssa, Bryan, and Jason are all single."

"Who's Jason?" Cathy asked, recognizing Alyssa and Bryan's names but wondering why Chantal had never before mentioned Jason.

"Jay is Chris's best friend who goes to a private school," Chantal replied. "He's really cute. Actually, like *really, really* cute. He's kind of a punk, though. He gives Jon a ton of crap about, well, everything, but mostly religion."

"Is he an atheist?" Cathy asked. "What school does he go to?"

"Ironically, he goes to St. Timothy's," Chantal responded with a small laugh. "So, I don't think he's an atheist. I think he just doesn't like church."

"That's weird," Cathy said, growing somewhat curious about him. "Maybe he just likes to get a rise out of Jon. After all, Jon is painfully serious."

Chantal threw a pillow at Cathy. "He's not serious; he's just passionate!" she laughed.

Cathy picked up the pillow and threw it back at her twin sister. "When are you hanging out with Jon's friends again?"

"Maybe tonight," Chantal replied. "I never thought you'd be interested in hanging out with us," she added after a short pause.

"Why not?"

"Jon's friends aren't like our friends from church," Chantal stated matter-of-factly. "Jon told me that some of them have been drunk before and some have smoked. They're just...kind of...I don't know...into trouble."

"Well, yeah, I knew that. Jon asked us to pray for them a while ago," Cathy recalled. "I know he wants to stay in their lives as a good influence. I can handle being around his friends."

CHAPTER 16

LATER THAT EVENING, CATHY felt a twinge of anxiety as she climbed into the passenger seat of her mother's car. She glanced at Chantal in the backseat; her shiny auburn hair fell perfectly straight past her shoulders, and a light coat of black mascara accentuated her emerald-green eyes. Wearing a purple sweater dress, black tights, and furry boots, she looked stunning.

Cathy glanced down at her own attire: a zip-up Boston Bruins hoodie, dark blue jeans, and snow boots—practical and functional, per usual. Her wavy auburn hair, which was slightly shorter than Chantal's, framed her makeup-less face. She had considered wearing eye-makeup, but she did not want to feel unauthentic. Lisa and Jon both saw Cathy regularly. She assumed that if she arrived at Chris's house all dressed up, then they would think that she was trying to impress them. The idea of ever appearing "fake" turned her stomach.

"I'm so excited you are going to meet everyone tonight!" Chantal exclaimed on their drive across Montgomery.

"Is that Jason-kid going to be there?" Cathy asked.

"No. He's skiing with his family this weekend," Chantal answered. "They have a house in Maine near Sugarloaf...and a beach house in Newport...and a mansion in Montgomery."

Cathy widened her eyes. "Wow," she said. "Sounds like Jason's family is loaded."

"Who's Jason?" Cathy's mother asked curiously. "One of Jon's friends?"

"Yeah. He goes to St. Timothy's, though, so Jon doesn't see him much," Chantal replied. "I've only met him once or twice."

"Why are you interested in meeting this boy, Cathy?" her mother asked and quickly glanced in her direction.

"No, it's not like that!" Cathy exclaimed with a laugh. "Chantal told me he's a jerk to Jon, so I was just wondering if I should be prepared to meet a punk."

"He's not mean. He just likes to tease people to make everyone laugh. Jon's an easy target because he's so innocent," Chantal explained. "All of Jon's friends are really nice."

"Is Chris's mom going to be home?" her mother inquired.

"Chris's older cousin, Jordan, is babysitting him and his little sister this weekend," Chantal replied. "Jordan's a senior at MLH. He's going to Notre Dame next year to play football. You can talk to him if you want."

"Chris's parents leave a senior in high school in charge of their home?" their mother questioned Chantal.

"All the time," Chantal replied. "Jordan's older brother, Taylor, stays there a lot too. He goes to Northeastern, though, so he's in Boston this weekend."

Mrs. Kagelli sighed. "Not the best parenting idea, but who am I to judge? Well, call me if anything gets out of hand or if you want me to pick you up early—and seriously, Chantal, don't drink any punch."

Chantal gasped. "Really? Did you have to go there?!"

"I'm kidding but be careful!" her mother retorted.

"I think Chantal learned her lesson with Andy," Cathy muttered as she exited the car.

A moment later, Cathy's heart thumped heavily against her chest as she stood with Chantal on Chris's front steps. The multiple cars in the driveway led Cathy to believe that Jordan had also invited friends over. She glanced at Chantal, who appeared as cheerful as usual, and wondered if she felt even the slightest bit nervous. Chantal was better than Cathy at adapting to new situations. In fact, meeting new people appeared to stimulate Chantal. Cathy, on the other hand, felt the need to size up situations before engaging in them.

Seconds later, the front door swung open, revealing Jon Anderson. Cathy instantly relaxed.

"Hi, Tal!" an attractive, well-built boy exclaimed from beside Lisa Ankerman on the nearby couch. "What's up, Chantal's twin?"

"This is Cathy," Chantal introduced her, as she paused in the middle of the room. "Cathy, you know Lisa, but this is Chris," she said and motioned towards the boy.

"Nice to meet you," Chris said in a friendly tone. "Thanks for coming over. Hopefully, we won't scare you away too quickly. If you guys want anything to eat or drink, help yourselves in the kitchen. Jordan ordered a bunch of pizzas and appetizers. He's downstairs in the basement with a few of his friends watching the Bruins game. I don't suggest going down there."

Cathy lowered her eyebrows in thought, wondering what Chris was implying. "Do I look like a hockey-phobe to you?" she asked dryly.

Chris smirked. "By the look of your fantastic black and gold attire, I'm pretty sure you can handle the Bruins/Habs game—the intensity of my cousin's stupidity, I'm not so sure."

"We have the game on, too," Jon said and sat down on the loveseat. "It's just in between periods."

"Cathy, come sit with me!" Lisa cried and patted the couch cushion beside her. "I've barely seen you in school lately. I'm so glad you came!"

"I'll grab you a drink," Chantal said to Cathy, while turning to leave the room. "What do you want?"

"Water's fine," Cathy replied and took a seat next to Lisa.

"You'll get to meet my friend Alyssa, who goes to Montgomery Lake Middle School with Jon and Chris," Lisa informed her. "Bryan Sartelli from Hamilton is on his way here, too. You'll love Bryan. He's one of the nicest guys I've ever met."

"Great," Cathy stated flatly, hoping Chantal would return soon. Although everyone was being friendly, she felt out of place. Historically, social situations brought Cathy more anxiety than pleasure, which was why she usually shied away from events that Chantal gladly attended. She had recently realized that her aversion to new situations could be a cause of the loneliness she felt. It was a catch twenty-two: she wanted friends but despised opening herself up to others. Nevertheless, to find her place within Montgomery's social realm, she knew she needed to step out from Chantal's shadow and establish her own identity.

Right before the Bruins game resumed, Alyssa arrived at Chris's house. She let herself in without knocking, took off her stylish boots at the door, and flopped onto the floor in front of the loveseat by Jon and Chantal's feet. Clearly, she was comfortable in the environment. Chris did not offer her anything to drink or get out of his seat to greet her. Jon did not flinch when she sat down in front of him. Chantal was the only one who even seemed to notice her. Even so, Alyssa looked perfectly at home. Cathy stared at her for a moment, wondering if anyone was going to introduce them.

"Oh, Lyss!" Chantal suddenly cried out. "That's my sister, Cathy," she said and pointed toward her. "I finally got her to hang out with us!"

Alyssa turned toward Cathy and smiled. "Awesome," she said. "It's great to have another girl around. It was just the boys and me for way too long."

"Yeah, Lyss has somehow put up with Chris and me for years," Jon chimed in and pulled on Alyssa's ponytail.

Alyssa fixed her ponytail and rolled her eyes at Jon. "Nice to meet you," she said and locked her hazel eyes on Cathy.

Cathy swallowed the lump in her throat, envying Alyssa's familiarity with the people in the room. "Same," she stated and smiled ever so slightly.

"Bryan said he'll be here in a half-hour," Chris announced.

"What's taking him so long?" Jon asked. "He told me earlier that he was coming over right after dinner."

Chris laughed and draped his arm around Lisa. "I'm sure it has something to do with that girl from his school. It always does."

"Bryan has a thing for the mayor's youngest daughter, Courtney," Lisa explained, as she turned to face Cathy.

"Is she his girlfriend?" Cathy asked.

Lisa shrugged. "No one knows," she replied with a laugh. "He won't talk about it."

As odd as Bryan's behavior seemed to everyone else in the room, Cathy could understand it. She was a master at keeping her feelings to herself. It was not that she wanted to be secretive or that she had dishonest intentions; rather, she felt no desire to verbally expose things she highly valued because doing so made her feel vulnerable. "I'm sure he has a good reason," Cathy said.

Bryan arrived halfway through third period. Although the game was tied and truly captivating, Cathy could not help but glance frequently in his direction. He was one of the most beautiful people she had ever seen. His spiky brown hair, hazel-brown eyes, and casual but preppy attire highly appealed to her senses. Chantal had mentioned that Jon's friends were all cute, but Cathy had underestimated her claim.

CHAPTER 17

OVER THE NEXT MONTH, Cathy made a point to spend as much time with Chantal's friends as possible. Lisa, whom Cathy had once considered cold, had ironically become one of her favorite people. Typically, Cathy, Chantal, and Jon attended youth group at their church on Friday nights and then hung out with Jon's friends on Saturdays. Slowly, Cathy was growing accustomed to Chris's candor, Bryan's reserved nature, Alyssa's dramatic tendencies, and Lisa's witty sarcasm. She was yet to meet Jason, but her curiosity about him heightened each time his name was mentioned.

That Saturday evening, Lisa and Alyssa were planning to sleep over the Kagellis' house. Chris's cousins—Jordan and Taylor—were taking Chris, Jon, and Bryan to the Bruins game, so the girls had planned a fun night of their own. Chantal, who had become very close with Alyssa, still believed there was animosity between herself and Lisa because of Andy. Although Cathy disagreed, she could not deny that Lisa was much friendlier to her than Chantal. It was the first time in Cathy's life that someone had preferred her to her twin. Lisa's fondness of Cathy placated much of her anxiety.

When Cathy wandered into Chantal's bedroom that afternoon, she found her twin sifting through a pile of old DVDs.

"Hey," Chantal said without looking up from the movies. "What do you think Lyss and Lis will want to watch tonight after the game? Are we even going to watch the game?"

Cathy sat down on Chantal's bed and shrugged. "I think I'm the only one who really cares about hockey," she admitted.

"I'm up for whatever," Chantal said carelessly. A few seconds later she looked up at Cathy, appearing to be in deep thought. "Do you think hanging out with Jon's friends is pulling us away from God, at all?" she asked, sounding as though she had already given the topic some consideration.

"Huh?" Cathy asked, completely thrown off by the question.

"I used to spend a lot more time with kids from church before I became friends with Jon's friends," Chantal replied. "I haven't hung out with the youth group girls in months."

"I don't feel like we're doing anything wrong by spending time with people outside of church," Cathy stated. "Mom always says it's important to be bright lights in a dark world."

"True."

"But?"

"I'm worried about Chris's influence on Jon," Chantal admitted. "I adore Chris, but he has bad role models. Jon has always had a positive impact on him, and Chris has always respected Jon's beliefs, but I've noticed that, lately, Jon seems less concerned about Chris than usual."

"What do you mean?"

"He used to ask me to pray all the time for the guys, and he always seemed worried about Taylor and Jordan corrupting them. Lately, he hasn't mentioned anything like that to me. Even when I told Jon that Chris looked high last weekend, he shrugged it off."

"You could always ask Lisa," Cathy suggested. "I'm sure she would know if Chris smokes weed."

"I can't picture Chris smoking anything," Chantal said and shook her head. "He's an athlete. I don't know why he would jeopardize his lungs. He wants to follow right in Taylor's footsteps. Taylor is probably going to get drafted by the NFL."

"Yeah, but look at the example Taylor has set," Cathy retorted. "I've only met him once, but he wasn't sober. I don't think Taylor and Jordan are straightedge athletes. I think they enjoy playing football and the praises that come along with being stars. Marc is the only Dunkin who seems to have any foresight."

"I've never met Marc," Chantal said.

"Oh. Well, Marc is hot."

Chantal gasped. "I don't think I've ever heard you call a guy hot!"

Cathy blushed.

"Jon's told me a lot about Marc," Chantal said. "He said he looks up to him and that Marc looks out for Chris. I just wish Jon cared about it as much as he used to. I think he's becoming desensitized to everything because he's around it so much. Sure, you and I hang out at Chris's on Saturdays, but Jon goes over there almost every day."

"You should tell Jon what you just told me," Cathy suggested.

"Maybe... It will be interesting to hear what the girls say tonight."

"I'm glad we became friends with Alyssa and Lisa," Cathy remarked. "I finally feel like I fit in somewhere besides the soccer field."

"What do you mean, you finally fit in?"

"Our new friends include me in plans," Cathy stated matter-of-factly. "Our friends from church never invite me anywhere unless you are going. The kids at church make me feel like something is wrong with me."

"There is nothing wrong with you," Chantal remarked firmly.

Of course, you think that, Cathy thought. *You have to think that. You're my sister.*

"And I'm not just saying that to make you feel better," Chantal added.

"I've tried so hard to be perfect, but it has not won me any friends at church. I've never felt accepted by a group of kids until I met Jon's friends."

"I've always wanted your company!" Chantal protested.

"I'm not talking about our family," Cathy responded with a short laugh. "I'm referring to people who don't have to like me."

"I think a lot of people like you," Chantal stated. "If anything, I think people are afraid you don't like them. You come off so confident."

I can't believe I come off confident. "Andy Rosetti aside, I like most people," Cathy stated dryly.

Chantal rolled her eyes.

"Maybe I've just tried too hard to be everyone's idea of perfect," Cathy said, wondering if she was, in fact, seeking too much external validation.

"I can't believe you are being this hard on yourself!" Chantal cried. "You're an awesome athlete and a great student. You have everything going for you. If anything, the girls at church are probably just jealous of you."

"That's what Mom said."

"And now at school, you hang out with Lisa, who—let's be honest—is the most popular girl in our grade," Chantal remarked.

"Yeah, things are a lot better now," Cathy agreed.

"I believe if I'm true to myself, the right people will flock to me," Chantal said. "Don't sweat over the people who shy away—just be thankful for the ones who appreciate you for who you are. The ones who don't value you aren't worth your time."

"That's a good way to look at it," Cathy agreed, realizing she probably cared way too much about what other people thought of her. "I'm just glad you introduced me to Chris and everyone. It will be fun if we're all still friends in high school."

"The boys dream of that day: everyone under one roof," Chantal said. "Even Jason will be allowed to attend MLH if he does well enough at St. Timothy's. He made some bet with his parents."

"I can't believe I still haven't met that kid."

"I'm sure you will soon. According to Jon, Chris is planning a party for next weekend. Taylor is babysitting, and he's allowing Chris to invite everyone over."

"Taylor's really nice," Cathy remarked.

"Yeah. I think Taylor and Jordan both seem really nice, just like Chris, but Jon is scared of Jordan," Chantal said. "He said Jordan tried to date rape one of Marc's friends."

"That's insane!" Cathy cried, widening her eyes. "He drugged her?"

Chantal shrugged. "According to Jon, she was at the party with Jordan and suddenly got sick, so he took her up to Chris's room. Marc assumed Jordan drugged her because she doesn't drink. Marc used to date her and still liked her, so the situation ruined his and Jordan's relationship."

"What a mess!"

Chantal nodded.

"Okay, I know I called Marc hot, but Jordan is like cover-model hot. I can't imagine he'd have to drug a girl to get her to hook up with him," Cathy said skeptically.

Chantal shrugged. "That's just what I heard from Jon."

"Chris must see a lot of crazy stuff when his cousins babysit," Cathy concluded, finding herself rather curious about what Chris had already been exposed to.

CHAPTER 18

JON ANDERSON ARRIVED AT Chris's house around 5:00 that night, wearing his Patrice Bergeron jersey and favorite Bruins hat. Because Jon did not have an older brother and his father lived in California, he had never attended a Bruins game. When Mr. and Mrs. Dunkin had surprised the boys with tickets to the game, Jon had become ecstatic.

"My parents are never around, but at least they know how to give nice presents," Chris remarked while he, Jon, and Bryan waited in the living room for Taylor and Jordan to arrive.

"How long are they gone for this time?" Bryan asked.

Chris shrugged. "Long enough for me to have a party next weekend."

"Who are you inviting?" Jon asked, wondering exactly what Chris had in mind.

"I'm thinking our crew from school, the girls, you guys and Jay, and maybe Lisa's friends from Sterling," Chris replied.

Jon scowled. "Like Andy Rosetti and those kids?"

"Yeah. I think I have to, man," Chris said. "Sorry, dude. It's for Lisa, obviously. Andy probably won't come anyway. According to Lis, he's not over Chantal. I'm sure he hates you as much as you hate him."

Jon knew he couldn't dictate who came to Chris's party, but Andy was his least favorite person in Montgomery. Earlier that year, Andy had fervently pursued Chantal and then tricked her into drinking spiked punch at his friend's house. Although that took place before Jon had been dating her, the whole situation with Andy still irked him.

"Bryan, you should invite the mayor's daughter," Chris suggested with a smirk.

"Not a chance," Bryan replied with a laugh. "I'll come by after I hang out with her."

"I bet she's wicked hot," Chris said, most likely trying to get under Bryan's skin.

Bryan just smiled and refused to comment.

A few moments later, Taylor and Jordan walked through the front door and into the living room. Jordan had a brown paper bag in his hand, which he set down on the coffee table. "You boys ready to pre-game?!" he exclaimed and raised one eyebrow. His blue eyes glimmered with amusement. He reached into the bag and pulled out a sleeve of nips. "Nothing gets you going like Fireball."

Jon was sure he looked horrified.

"Sweet," Chris said.

Bryan stared at Jordan with wide eyes.

"J, if any of them puke, it's on you," Taylor stated, sounding less than enthused.

"One for each of you—that's it," Jordan said, as he tore the package open.

Jon felt his face turn red as his heart began to pound. He had never even drunk beer, let alone hard liquor! He was only thirteen!

"Jonny-A, you look horrified," Jordan remarked with a loud laugh. "It's just one shot. It'll warm you up, buddy. That's all. You won't even feel a buzz."

Chris, who was sitting beside Jon on the couch, nudged him in the shoulder. "It'll be fine, dude."

A second later, Jordan was standing in front of Jon, expecting him to take the miniature bottle of whiskey out of his hand. Jon felt everyone's eyes on him.

"Guy, you'll be fine," Bryan said and nodded at Jon.

Jon sighed and snatched the bottle out of Jordan's hand.

Chris began laughing. "Yes! That's awesome!"

Jon felt butterflies in his stomach. Even though his head was telling him not to drink it, he felt slightly excited.

"All right, open up your bottles," Jordan directed. "We're going to toast to Jon's first drink."

Jon's face felt so hot; he knew he must have been bright red.

"Cheers!" Chris exclaimed, holding his nip up in the air.

"Cheers," Jordan replied. "Now toss those back in one big gulp. Trust me; it burns a lot less that way."

Jon threw back the shot in one fluid motion. He did exactly what Jordan said, but it burned. It burned! "Ugh!" he exclaimed and bolted into the kitchen to grab water. He could hear Chris laughing loudly from the living room. "Stop!" he yelled.

When he walked back into the room, Chris started clapping. "I'm so proud of you, buddy."

Jon sighed. *That's always a bad sign.*

CHAPTER 19

"JON, I AM IN shock. I don't even know what to say," Chantal stated over the phone the following morning. "I need to process what you just told me."

Jon was sitting alone at Chris's kitchen table, trembling on the other end of the line. "Chantal, please talk this through with me," he pleaded. "I'm stuck at Chris's house without a ride to church. Everyone else is still asleep and probably will be for hours. My mom can't pick me up because she's at my sister's soccer practice. They are going straight to church from the field. I was supposed to walk home before eight to go with them, but I didn't wake up until nine."

"This is why spending time with Chris's cousins is bad!" Chantal exclaimed. "They pressured you into drinking, and now you're going to miss church."

Jon sighed. "Taking one shot at 5:30 last night had nothing to do with me oversleeping," he retorted. "We stayed up playing Xbox after we got home. I forgot to set an alarm. That's it."

"I can't deal with this right now," Chantal stated coldly. "Lisa and Alyssa are here. I still have to eat and get ready. I'll call you later."

"Can we hang out this afternoon?" Jon asked.

"I don't know," Chantal said flatly. "I'll call you later."

Jon's heart pounded. "You know, I didn't have to tell you about this," he stated defensively. "We should be able to be honest with each other and talk things out. It's not like I got drunk! I had one shot, which was basically forced on me by an eighteen-year-old."

"I'll call you later," Chantal repeated before hanging up on him.

***

After a few days of back and forth banter, Chantal finally forgave Jon for his "misdeed." However, just because she forgave him did not mean she was open to attending Chris's party that coming weekend. After learning that Taylor and Jordan had "made" the boys drink hard liquor, she was afraid it would happen again. In the meantime, Lisa was trying to convince Cathy to attend the party with or without Chantal.

"I love hanging out with you, Chris, and everyone. I just don't feel that comfortable around the older kids," Cathy explained to Lisa during lunch on Friday.

"We don't have to spend time with Chris's cousins," Lisa replied. "My friends Leslie and Katherine from cheerleading are coming. Katherine is the shiest person I know. She'll *definitely* want to avoid the older kids. I really want you to meet her and Leslie. Plus, Alyssa will be there and so will Bryan and Jon. You'll feel comfortable."

"Are Taylor and Jordan both going to be there?" Cathy asked.

Lisa shook her head. "No. Jordan's going to a concert. It's just Taylor this time."

"Taylor's nice."

Lisa nodded. "They're both nice. Why don't you come over my house tomorrow and get ready for the party with me? You can borrow one of my outfits. I'll even do your makeup if you want. You will look stunning."

Cathy liked the idea of spending one-on-one time with Lisa because she wanted a best friend besides Chantal. She knew becoming closer with Lisa would help her fit in better, and that was what she desired more than anything.

CHAPTER 20

*T*ONIGHT COULD GO DOWN *in history as one of my favorite nights of all,* Cathy thought as she glanced at the people surrounding her in Chris's living room the following evening.

Jordan and his high school friends were out of town, so Taylor had allowed Chris to invite a lot of kids his age. The party represented the joining of all seventh-grade forces. Students from all three Montgomery middle schools—Sterling, Montgomery Lake, and Hamilton—were present, and Cathy felt blessed to be there. Best of all, she had been invited there by a friend, not her sister.

Taylor was adamant that no middle school kids drank alcohol at the party. The college kids, however, were fully engaged in drinking games. In the kitchen, flip-cup was set up; in the living room, circle of death was taking place; and in the basement, a beer-pong tournament was underway.

"Cathy, this is Katherine," Lisa said, introducing her to a tiny brunette with hazel-gray eyes. Cathy thought she looked about ten-years-old. "She's the best cheerleader on my squad."

"Nice to meet you," Cathy said and smiled at Katherine.

"You too," Katherine replied.

"I'll introduce you to Leslie once she's done talking to Bobby and Adam," Lisa said and nodded toward a blonde, who was vivaciously chatting with Bobby Ryan and Adam Case—boys in Cathy's grade at Sterling.

"I don't know how she does that," Katherine commented with a small laugh. "She hardly knows them."

"Leslie could start a conversation with a stone wall," Lisa remarked.

"Want to play a game, you guys?" Chris asked as he walked over to Cathy and the girls.

"Sure," Lisa and Cathy said in unison while Katherine remained silent.

"Cool. Lisa, come upstairs with me for a minute," Chris said and tugged on her arm. "I need your help with something."

"O-kay," Lisa sang and allowed Chris to drag her toward the nearby staircase. They returned a moment later, just as Chantal and Jon walked through the front door.

"Oh, sweet! You guys are just in time for Mafia," Chris said and slapped hands with Jon. "Help yourself to snacks and drinks in the kitchen. We're heading into the dining room."

As Chantal and Jon ventured into the kitchen, Cathy, Lisa, and Katherine followed Chris out of the room. Leslie, Adam, Bobby, Alyssa, Chantal, and Jon joined them in the dining room a moment later. Chris put a deck of cards on the table and began explaining the rules of a game called Mafia. It took just one round for Cathy to become completely hooked on the game. It was all about persuasion, critical thinking, and reading people. She loved it, and she was good at it.

Bryan arrived halfway through the second round—without the mayor's daughter, just as everyone had expected. After a few rounds of the game, Cathy noticed Lisa becoming rather giddy and Chris growing louder and louder. Cathy looked at Lisa's cup, wondering what Chris had put in it when they went upstairs.

A few moments later, Taylor walked into the dining room. He was wearing a black wife-beater tank-top that accentuated his V-shape torso and muscular arms. He had the best body Cathy had ever seen. "What are you kids up to?" he asked and patted Chris on the shoulder. "No drinking, right?"

Chris smiled innocently.

Taylor winked. "Have fun," he said and turned out of the room.

"Is he not letting you drink?" Bryan asked once Taylor was out of hearing distance.

Chris held up his cup and wiggled it in the air. "I'm taken care of."

"So, he's just not letting any of us drink?" Bryan gathered.

"It's Jordan who usually instigates that," Chris replied. "Taylor's cautious because we're, like, eight years younger than him. Jordan left rum in my room. Go make a drink."

"For real?" Bryan asked.

"Yeah, it's on my bureau," Chris replied. "Any of you can go up there. Jordan's the man."

"Jon, come with me," Bryan said as he stood up.

Jon stood up slowly. "I'll come, but I don't want a drink."

"Oh, c'mon, Jonny-boy!" Chris exclaimed. "We popped your cherry last weekend."

Chantal turned toward Jon with sheer fire in her eyes. Cathy had never seen her twin look so angry. This should have been enough to bring Jon back to his seat, but surprisingly, he followed Bryan out of the room. Cathy highly doubted Jon would drink, but by going upstairs with Bryan, he certainly hadn't denounced the idea. *This is getting interesting.*

CHAPTER 21

A FEW MOMENTS LATER, CHANTAL let out a loud sigh of relief when Jon entered the room empty handed. Even so, Cathy could tell her sister was upset. Of course, she was—she expected Jon to have the same convictions he had when they first began dating and he was ardently against drugs and alcohol. Chantal whispered something into Jon's ear and stood up from the table. Jon looked up at her strangely before slowly rising.

"We'll be right back," Chantal said flatly and hustled out of the room. Jon looked slightly embarrassed when he turned to follow her into the hallway.

"Okay, so while they go have an awkward conversation, we're going to play another round," Chris said. He let out a short laugh and began passing cards to everyone.

Cathy hoped she would be dealt an Ace, so she could be one of the mafia members. "Being mafia" meant she'd have to trick everyone into believing she was innocent. She had been mafia during the second match, and she had loved the challenge. This time, however, Cathy was dealt a king, which made her the sheriff. That meant she would have to play detective and figure out who the mafia members were before they "killed" her.

Cathy and her friends were more than halfway through the game when Jon walked back into the room without Chantal. He was just in time to hear Cathy share everything she had deduced. "So, I'm the sheriff," she blurted out, "and I checked Katherine during the first round. She is mafia. I checked Leslie during this round; she is not mafia."

Leslie let out a sigh of relief. "I'm glad to hear you say that."

"So, I'm likely dead next round because Alyssa was the medic, and she isn't alive to protect me," Cathy reasoned. "So, I have to lay out everything I know for you guys right now. Bryan, Alyssa, and Bobby are dead, so I believe they were all innocent. Since Katherine is mafia and Lisa stood up for her earlier, I'm leaning toward Lisa being the other mafia member more so than Adam. I formally accuse Katherine of being mafia."

"I second that!" Adam exclaimed. "I'm not mafia."

Cathy smiled, she loved putting puzzles together.

"Okay, let's take a vote," Chris said. "Who thinks Katherine is mafioso?"

Cathy, Adam, and Leslie all raised their hands.

"Sorry, Katherine," Chris said and shook his head. "You're gone. Town of Montgomery go to sleep..."

Chris went through all the usual motions. Cathy checked Lisa: she was, in fact, mafia. When Chris woke up the town, he surprised Cathy by saying Adam had died.

Hmmm... a curve ball. By killing Adam instead of me, Lisa must be trying to convince Leslie that I was lying and that I'm actually mafia. "I formally accuse Lisa of being mafia," Cathy announced as soon as Chris was done telling Adam's death story. "She didn't kill me, just so I would look guilty. I checked her this round, and she is definitely mafia."

"Lis, your rebuttal?" Chris inquired.

"Cathy is mafia. Alyssa was her teammate. Bryan was probably the real sheriff," Lisa stated, looking directly at Leslie. "Katherine was the medic, and you've just been fooled this entire time."

Leslie widened her eyes and took a deep breath. She glanced back and forth from Lisa to Cathy.

"Katherine was the first person I checked," Cathy stated. "She was *definitely* mafia, which means Alyssa was the real medic; Bryan, you, and Bobby are all townspeople; and I'm the sheriff. I checked you, and that's how I know we are on the same team. If we vote Lisa off, we win the game."

"It's time to vote," Chris interjected. "Who thinks my GF is a hitwoman?"

Cathy raised her hand immediately and stared at Leslie.

Leslie bit her bottom lip and then slowly raised her hand. "Sorry, Lis."

Lisa groaned.

"The town wins!" Chris exclaimed.

"Yay!!" Leslie cried.

"You're good at this," Chris said to Cathy. "You'll have to play sometime when my friend Jay is here. He's such a 'lawyer.' He's the one who taught me how to play. He would love to get a rise out of you."

"Ah, the phantom Jason I'm yet to meet," Cathy replied. "I would welcome the competition."

"He's smart," Chris said. "Very smart."

"Why isn't he ever around?" Cathy asked.

"He goes away skiing with his family all the time," Chris replied. "He also has a ton of homework. St. Timothy's isn't an easy school, and he's determined to get straight A's."

"I'm sure I'll meet him someday."

"He'd like that," Chris said with a smirk. His expression made Cathy wonder if Jason had already heard about her.

"Mafia is even fun to watch," Jon said, interrupting Cathy's thoughts as he stepped between her and Chris. "Cathy, Chantal's in the kitchen. She wants to talk to you."

"Is everything okay?" Cathy asked, sending Jon a perplexed look.

Jon shrugged.

Cathy stood up. "I'll go," she said and left the room. She found Chantal standing by the kitchen door with her arms crossed and her head down. "What's going on?"

"I'm really upset, and I want to leave," Chantal stated matter-of-factly.

Cathy could see frustration in her eyes. "Why?" she asked.

Chantal sighed. "I was nice enough to forgive Jon for drinking last weekend. I never expected him to condone Bryan's drinking, tonight! He doesn't think he did anything wrong, and he can't see how bad it looks."

"He didn't come back with a drink, so he probably can't understand why you are so upset over him going upstairs," Cathy reasoned.

"I told him on the walk here that I was worried he was becoming desensitized," Chantal explained. "He said he didn't want to rain on Chris's parade, but he wasn't going to join in."

"Honestly, I think you're worried Jon is going to get corrupted by his friends," Cathy said. "If you weren't afraid, you wouldn't care that he went upstairs with Bryan."

"You're right!" Chantal exclaimed. "I am worried about him. He's acting weird."

Jon was acting out of character, but Cathy assumed he was just trying to please everyone. That was an impossible task when Chris and Bryan wanted him to drink and Chantal wanted him to stay sober. Jon was in a tough spot. "Chantal, you should probably make him feel good about his decision not to drink and show him that he has your support. It's not easy to let down your friends. If you stay mad at him over this, he will probably give up on trying to please you and try to please them."

"How can I pretend I'm not mad when I am?"

"You're not mad; you're scared."

"I'm mad."

Cathy scowled. "Look, I don't know what else to say except I think you should let this go and enjoy the rest of the night. Jon didn't drink."

"I called Mom and asked her to pick me up," Chantal stated.

"I don't think you should leave," Cathy warned. "If Jon thinks you're upset with him, he will be more apt to drink. You need to support him."

Chantal shook her head. "I can't do that. I have to hold him accountable. He can't claim to be against alcohol and then not stand up to his friends. It doesn't work like that."

"Mom is fine with coming back to pick me up?" Cathy asked, realizing that reasoning with Chantal was not going to get her anywhere. Their minds worked differently. Cathy always considered the likely outcome and based her decisions on that. Chantal based her decisions on her personal feelings. For that reason, neither twin could easily talk the other into anything.

Chantal nodded.

"What exactly did you say to Jon?"

"I told him I'm uncomfortable with his decision to condone drinking, so I want to go home."

"What did he say?"

"He said I was overreacting and that he didn't condone anything."

Cathy could understand why Chantal was concerned, but she agreed with Jon. "I don't think leaving here will make anything better."

"I see headlights," Chantal said, as she peered out the window next to the kitchen door. "I think that's Mom. I'm going to check."

Cathy stepped out on the porch and watched Chantal get into their mother's white car. *You just made a huge mistake.*

CHAPTER 22

"**D**ID CHANTAL JUST LEAVE?" Lisa asked once Cathy returned to the dining room where her friends had remained.

"Yeah," Cathy replied downheartedly and took her seat between Lisa and Katherine.

"Aww, no, really?" Chris asked, sounding upset. "Oh @#$%! I feel bad now."

"Yeah, I do, too," Bryan stated and turned toward Jon. "Is it because you came upstairs with me?"

"It's *not* your fault," Jon stressed. "She's upset with me. She's been like this all week. I'm surprised she even came tonight."

"If she's mad at you, then she must be pissed at me!" Chris exclaimed and widened his blue eyes.

Jon shook his head. "It's completely between me and her."

"Well, I'm sorry, dude," Chris said.

"Thanks," Jon said, sounding dejected.

"We need to lighten the mood," Leslie commented, glancing from Jon to Chris. "Any ideas?"

"Shots?" Chris joked and winked at her.

Leslie rolled her green eyes and laughed.

"Let's go see what's going on in the other room," Chris suggested and stood up from his chair. "Maybe there's another game we can get in on. Who knows? Maybe Taylor's 'relaxed' enough to let us join the festivities."

Chris led them into the living room where Taylor and a half dozen of his friends were still playing circle of death. There was a large pile of empty beer cans on the floor near the table, which led Cathy to believe it was a heavy drinking game—one Taylor would never allow them to play.

"What's up, Little D?" Taylor called out once he noticed Chris across the room.

"Nothing. Just seeing what you guys are up to."

"Circle of death, buddy," Taylor said. "Go see if they'll let you play a round of flip-cup with soda."

"Okay," Chris replied and turned back toward his friends. "Bryan and Lisa, come upstairs with me for a minute. Anyone else want a drink?"

Silence.

"Okay, we'll BRB," Chris said, turning toward the stairs.

Once Chris, Bryan, and Lisa disappeared up the stairs, Cathy turned to Jon. "Are you okay? We can go talk somewhere if you want."

"She's making me feel like crap," Jon admitted quietly to Cathy. "I can't reason with her."

Cathy shook her head. "I can't either."

"I went upstairs with my friend," Jon stated flatly. "There's nothing wrong with that."

Cathy felt bad. Jon didn't deserve Chantal's wrath for simply escorting Bryan to Chris's room. "I told her she should stay and be supportive of your decision not to drink."

"Right?" Jon agreed. "I turned down alcohol, let down my friends, and she left the party. It's so backwards." The longer they spoke, the angrier he sounded.

"Chantal doesn't understand what it's like to feel external pressure. She bases everything on what *she* feels is right. Other people's opinions don't phase her. She has no idea that it took strength to turn down Chris's offer because turning people down is easy for her," Cathy said, attempting to describe her twin's personality.

"I can see that."

"The only way to deal with her when she gets like this is to give her space. When her 'upset' feelings die down, she will miss you. That will move her to make up with you," Cathy continued.

"It's so frustrating!" Jon exclaimed and let out a heavy sigh. "I hate it when anyone is upset with me. I can't even sleep when I'm in a fight with someone I care about."

"I'm really sorry you're going through this," Cathy said and put her head down.

"Thanks. You're good to talk to. I miss—"

"—Hey! Jonny-boy!" Chris called as he and Bryan approached Jon and Cathy. "We've decided that you just had a really crappy thing happen to you, so you deserve a drink. We made a nice and strong one for ya!" He handed a red solo cup to Jon. "Your girl got mad at you for *not* drinking, so that means you should probably *start* drinking."

Cathy widened her eyes. She had expected this very thing to happen.

"You know what? If this will calm me down, then bottoms up," Jon said and threw back his cup.

Yup, saw that coming.

Jon chugged the entire cup.

Didn't see that coming.

"Great. Now chill!" Chris laughed and patted him on the back. "Time for a new game."

"Then I'm going to need a refill," Jon said and shook his empty cup.

Chris looked slightly taken aback. "Welcome to the party, bud!" he cried.

Cathy must have looked like a deer in headlights while staring at Jon because Lisa rushed over to her. "Is everything okay?" she asked and lowered her eyebrows in a perplexed manor.

"*Oh my gosh,*" Cathy said and covered her mouth to stop herself from laughing. "This is so ironic!" After a few seconds, she couldn't keep herself from laughing out loud. "They're going to get Jon wasted, and none of this would have happened if Chantal had stayed at the party."

"Jon drank that?" Lisa gasped. "Chris filled it halfway with rum. He was just hoping Jon would take a sip!"

Cathy laughed again. She didn't know why she was finding the situation so amusing, but she loved the irony. Perhaps it was because she had called it... or maybe because Chantal had been too stubborn to take her advice... or possibly because she thought it could teach Chantal a lesson.

"I'm surprised you're taking this so lightly," Lisa commented and cocked her head to the side. "You're so against drinking, but you're laughing."

"It's the irony," Cathy stated and shook her head. "Chantal got so mad over the possibility of him drinking that her wrath caused him to drink."

"It *is* pretty ironic," Lisa agreed. "If she finds out about this, do you think she'll break up with him?"

"Maybe."

"Well I know one person who would be happy about that," Lisa said, clearly referring to Andy.

Ugh. "I don't know what to think anymore," Cathy sighed. "I thought Jon was better for her because he shared her values, but he's losing them pretty quickly. She's not helping matters either."

"Yeah... well... enough about them. I'm starting to get depressed. Let's go play flip-cup," Lisa said and linked arms with Cathy.

When the girls walked into the kitchen, the college kids were finishing up a game. Cathy was happy to watch some of it before playing. People were lined up on either side of the kitchen table with solo cups in front of them. Flip-cup was a relay-race to see which side of the table could finish their drinks and flip their cups over first. It required balance, which many of the college kids were lacking due to alcohol, so it was hilarious watching them try to win.

Katherine, Alyssa, Leslie, Bobby, Adam, and Bryan were standing nearby, watching the competition with amusement. Chris and Jon entered the kitchen a moment later with fresh drinks in their hands and then made their way over to Lisa and Cathy.

"Do you want some of this in your cup?" Chris asked Lisa.

"Noooo," Lisa stressed and shook her head. "I don't want to get sick."

"Gotcha," Chris said. "What time are you leaving, Cathy?"

"In an hour," Cathy replied.

"Do you want to sleep over my house so you can stay later?" Lisa offered.

"Sure, if my mom will let me!" Cathy replied, loving the idea.

Cathy was ecstatic when her mother agreed to the sleepover. She was looking forward to not only spending more time with Lisa, but also avoiding her overly emotional sister.

CHAPTER 23

A ROUND 10:30 P.M., MARC entered his cousin Chris's large colonial home with his friends Pat Ryan, Ricky Samson, and Robby Rosetti. The house seemed rather still, which was odd considering Taylor was housesitting. In the kitchen, Marc saw a group of Chris's friends and began to wonder where all of Taylor's friends were. After wiping snow off his feet, he walked over to the kitchen table. "Where's Chris?" he asked.

Jon pointed his finger up toward the ceiling.

"With his girl," Bryan replied.

Marc let out a short laugh. Thirteen-year-old Chris had a better sex life than half of Marc's friends. "It's so quiet up here. Is everyone else downstairs?" he inquired, locking his light blue eyes on Cathy. Her slightly-longer-than-shoulder-length auburn hair framed her face beautifully, and at that moment, he found himself wishing she was closer to his age.

"I think so," she replied. "There's a beer pong tournament going on down there. Some kids might still be in the living room."

"Thanks," Marc said and smiled. "Cathy, right?"

Cathy nodded, appearing surprised that he knew her name. He had seen her at Chris's house on a few occasions, but they had only been formally introduced once.

"Whose beers are those on the table?" Marc asked, glancing strangely at everyone. "T didn't let you guys drink, did he?" he was sure he looked horrified by the thought.

"He gave them to us for flip cup after he caught us playing with rum," Bryan responded.

Marc dropped his jaw. "Where the heck did you get rum?!"

"Jordan, supposedly," Bryan stated. "Taylor wasn't going to let Chris drink, but Jordan left some rum in his room."

Marc shook his head and sighed. "I don't know what's wrong with him."

Suddenly, Jon raced out of the kitchen, unannounced, holding his stomach.

"What's wrong with Anderson?" Marc asked.

"Chris got him drunk," Bryan responded with a short laugh.

"What?!" Marc exclaimed.

Bryan nodded. "Jonny shocked us all."

Marc was troubled by everything he was hearing. "Who's staying over?"

"Me and Jon," Bryan replied.

"Thank God," Marc said. "How are you getting home, Cathy?"

"I'm going with Lisa," she replied.

"Cool. Well, I have to find T. When Chris comes out of his bedroom, tell him I want to talk to him," Marc said, glancing from Cathy to Bryan.

"You got it," Bryan replied. "We'll come downstairs after everyone else leaves."

***

A couple of hours later in Chris's finely finished basement, Marc observed the scene before him. To his left, Chris and Bryan were sitting by the TV with a few of Taylor's friends. To his right, the fourth round of a beer pong tournament was underway. The competition had started long before Marc arrived with sixteen teams, playing eight matchups on two different tables. Everyone paid a ten-dollar entrance fee, so the winning team stood to earn over three hundred dollars.

From upon his barstool, Marc watched Taylor effortlessly sink ping-pong ball after ping-pong ball into his opponents' cups. Taylor's hand-eye coordination was unmatched. Marc could tell he was taking the competition quite seriously. He looked as focused as he typically did on a football field. Assuming Taylor had been drinking all night, Marc found it strange that he appeared sober; his balance and aim were perfect.

"How's it going?" Chris asked, interrupting Marc's contemplation as he appeared beside him with Bryan.

"T's dominating the game," Marc replied and nodded toward the beer pong table.

"Nice."

"Have you checked on Jon lately?"

"Last time I did, he was passed out in the bathroom," Chris replied. "I can't believe he drank tonight. He was on a mission to spite Chantal, I think."

Marc was just as shocked as Chris. He knew Chris's friends well, and Jon was the most innocent. "Keep checking on him. No seventh grader should be puking up rum."

"I'll be surprised if Jon ever drinks again," Bryan commented.

"Jordan shouldn't have left you that bottle," Marc stated firmly. "He'll answer to Taylor for that."

"It's all good," Chris said and turned away from Marc. "We're going outside for a bit, but we'll be back."

"Wait," Marc called. "What's outside at 1:00 A.M.?"

Chris turned around. "Don't worry about it," he replied, gesturing for Bryan to follow him to the door. Marc assumed they were going outside to smoke. Over the last six months, he had caught Chris smoking enough times to realize it was becoming a habit. Despite the imminent risks, Taylor, Jordan, and Chris's parents didn't seem too concerned. They all wrote it off as a phase.

Standing up from his barstool, Marc moved closer to the beer pong tournament. The fourth round had started with fifteen cups on each end instead of the typical ten. In front of Taylor and his teammate, Ryan Blake, eight cups remained. At their opponents' end, only three cups were left. After Taylor and Ryan both sunk their shots, they were granted a chance to try for the last cup. Everyone in the basement crowded around the table.

The pressure was on—but Taylor always thrived under pressure. No one was surprised when his carefully thrown ping-pong ball landed inside the last cup. Considering the other team's apparent drunkenness, it was no shock when they failed to rebuttal. "That's game!" Taylor exclaimed and threw his hands triumphantly in the air. "Championship in twenty!" he was smiling from ear to ear when Marc approached him at the table.

"What's up?" Taylor greeted him. "Did your friends all leave?"

Marc nodded. "Most of them have midnight curfews."

"Do you want to play a round?" Taylor proposed, tossing a ping-pong ball at Marc.

Marc caught it and walked to the other end of the table. "If we have time," he replied.

"We have time," Taylor said. "Everyone else went upstairs to get more beer or outside to smoke."

"You know who else went outside to smoke? Chris."

"Weed?" Taylor asked, looking alarmed.

"No, cigarettes," Marc clarified.

Taylor waved off Marc. "Oh, I wouldn't worry about that. He'll stop like Jordan did once he sees what it does to his game."

"When did Jordan ever smoke?" Marc inquired. He had partied with his brothers enough to know that neither one of them smoked cigarettes—not even when they were drunk.

Taylor laughed. "For all of one week when he was a punk freshman and thought he was wicked cool. I only knew because he asked me to buy them for him. Instead, I made him run twenty laps around the football field. Needless to say, he never smoked again."

"So that's why you're not worried about Chris? You think he'll put football first like Jordan?"

"Smoking butts doesn't make anyone a better athlete. It's like ingesting poison. He'll stop."

"Maybe."

Taylor shrugged. "If he wants to win, he'll learn how to discipline himself. If he gets some things out of his system now, he'll be more focused in high school. That's when it will matter. The kid was already the captain of his Montgomery team. He'll be the captain again next year. It's his offseason right now."

"Talk to him," Marc pressed. "He takes nothing seriously."

"I'll deal with him. He just walked back inside with Bryan. Let's see if they want to play with us. We can play with water." Taylor caught Chris's attention and waved him over.

"S'up?" Chris asked once he reached the table.

"Where have you been?" Taylor inquired.

"Outside with your friends."

Taylor looked back and forth from Chris and Bryan. He took a step back and squinted. "Are you...high?" he asked, seconds later while widening his blue eyes.

Chris immediately started laughing.

"Not cool, dude!" Taylor stated and shook his head. "I don't mind you having a beer, but weed should not be in play."

Chris looked up at Taylor, appearing completely unfazed.

"I'll find out who let you smoke, and I'll make sure it doesn't happen again," Taylor said. "Don't make me regret allowing you down here."

Chris shrugged. "Sorry. Bryan and I were already outside when your friends came out. They started passing around a bowl, and some drunk kid passed it my way. I didn't go looking for it."

"It doesn't matter. You've got to tone it down," Taylor stated emphatically.

"O-kay," Chris sang, sounding rather careless.

"You're in *seventh grade*. I didn't drink until I was a junior in high school," Taylor said, "and weed came much later."

"Yeah? Well, what about everything else?" Chris retorted and raised his eyebrows at Taylor.

Taylor looked down at the red solo cup he was setting on the table. "I don't know what you're talking about, buddy."

"Your friends were telling a story outside about a huge beer pong tournament you won in Boston," Chris said with a smirk.

Marc could tell by the look on Taylor's face that the story was going to be incriminating.

"They said everyone was so drunk that there wouldn't have been a championship round if you hadn't laid out lines of coke for the players," Chris recounted, sounding amused. "According to them, you like coke."

Holy crap! Marc darted his eyes from Chris to Taylor.

Taylor started laughing. "Are you seriously bringing up something you heard I did in college to defend what you just did as a seventh grader?"

Chris shook his head. "No. I just want to know when you started doing all the drugs you do."

Taylor looked stunned by Chris's brash statement. "All the drugs I do?" he asked, widening his eyes. "The only drug I 'do' regularly is beer—if you want to call that a drug. I smoke weed if I'm sore after a tough workout. I can't say there's anything else in play."

"So, college then."

"What?"

"The answer to my question is when you were in college," Chris stated matter-of-factly.

"Why don't you and Bryan go check on Jon," Marc suggested to Chris, hoping to break up the tension between him and Taylor.

"Yeah, do that," Taylor directed. "Marc and I want to play a round of beer pong before the tournament starts back up. Go check on Jon and go to bed."

Chris sighed.

"Go," Taylor repeated and pointed toward the stairs.

Chris rolled his eyes and turned away from Taylor and Marc. Bryan followed Chris, looking somewhat ashamed.

"He has guts," Marc said once Chris was out of hearing distance.

"He's a little $@#&!" Taylor exclaimed. "You were worried about him smoking butts, and he was outside smoking weed! We have to reign this kid in!"

"Then you have to talk to Jordan. He buys Chris everything he wants."

Taylor rolled his eyes. "Jordan's not gonna care. He just wants to be Chris's favorite cousin. It's a manifestation of his middle-child syndrome."

Marc laughed. "Actually, you're probably right."

"Jordan won't be any help, but if Chris doesn't chill, I'll talk to Uncle Mike and Aunty Jen."

"Do you think they'll do anything?"

Taylor shrugged. "I don't know, but it's worth a try. Maybe they can ground him or something. I have no idea how to parent."

"I don't think they do either," Marc said dryly. He loved his aunt and uncle but felt they had no business having children. They were co-owners of an international consulting firm based in London. This demanded abroad travel each month for weeks at a time. Consequently, a live-in nanny had cared for Chris and Katie throughout most of their childhood. Once Chris was old enough to babysit Katie, their parents released the nanny and asked Taylor to housesit whenever they traveled. When Taylor couldn't make it home from college, Jordan took the responsibility. Katie frequently stayed with Marc's parents, but Taylor and Jordan were basically raising Chris.

"If I were home more, I would get Chris on a fitness regimen and hold him accountable," Taylor said. "Can you do something like that for him?"

Marc was relieved that Taylor seemed concerned. "Yeah, if you'll help me design one."

"I can do that."

"He has a lot of influence on his friends. Jon's upstairs puking. Bryan's as high as Chris. They're three years younger than me, dude. They're way too young."

"Hopefully, Chris forgets what we just talked about. Thinking I party all the time with coke won't encourage him to stay in line."

"Is everything really just occasional, T?"

"Absolutely," Taylor assured him. "I mean, that story Chris heard is true, but I don't have a problem with coke. It's completely sporadic."

"You guys party a lot with ecstasy, though, right?"

"We used to go to clubs and raves before everyone turned twenty-one. Now that we can all drink, we just go to Faneuil Hall. I haven't rolled since, I think, last year."

Knowing addiction ran in his family had been enough to keep Marc away from experimenting with drugs. For years, he had assumed Taylor and Jordan felt the same way, but as he got older, he realized his brothers had much less conviction. He had never expected Taylor, who had always been a focused student-athlete, to get caught up in Boston's club scene. For years, Taylor had been the role model for every aspiring athlete in town. In people's minds, he was still destined for the NFL, but Marc could tell that his focus had waned.

"Do you still want to play?" Taylor asked, holding a ping-pong ball up in the air.

"If there's time."

Taylor smirked. "There's time. I just have to grab some more beer upstairs. Hang tight."

CHAPTER 24

"ANDERSON, WAKE UP!" CHRIS shouted, nudging his passed-out friend in the shoulder. Jon was lying sprawled out diagonally across Chris's king-sized bed. "Wake up, dude."

"Looks like you're sleeping on the futon tonight," Bryan said with a laugh.

"Hell no," Chris stated. He reached underneath Jon's back and rolled him over to the right side of the bed. "I'll sleep with him if I have to, but he's not taking up my entire bed. You get the futon," he said and threw Bryan a pillow. "Grab some extra blankets out of my closet. I'm going downstairs to get water and a puke bucket for Jon."

As Chris stumbled his way downstairs, he laughed in disbelief that Jon—his most uptight friend—was the first one to get sick at a party. After jumping off the bottom step, Chris turned left into his oversized, country kitchen. Taylor and his friend Ryan were standing by the mahogany cabinets near the fridge, and they looked downright startled to see Chris enter the room.

"What are you doing down here?" Taylor asked, widening his eyes like a deer staring into oncoming headlights.

"Um, getting water and a puke bucket for Jon," Chris replied and continued walking toward the refrigerator. "What are you doing?"

Taylor stared at him blankly, and Chris realized he was at a loss for words. Chris darted his eyes toward the granite countertop only to see a small, open bag of white powder. Chris widened his blue eyes and dropped his jaw. He could not believe he had just caught his cousin, red-handed, with cocaine. He laughed. "You guys have an awful lot of baby powder right there. I'm sure that will sober you right up so you can win the tournament."

Taylor brought both of his hands to his mouth and closed his eyes. "$@#%," he muttered beneath his breath.

"My bad," Ryan said and picked the bag up off the counter. "This is mine, not his."

Chris grabbed a bottle of water out of the fridge and laughed. "Good luck, guys. Excuse me," he said nonchalantly as he reached past Taylor to grab a bucket out of a cabinet.

When Chris looked up, Taylor was still resting his head in his hands, as though he couldn't bring himself to look at his younger cousin. As he turned to leave the room, Taylor called out, "We'll talk about this tomorrow. Neither one of us is in the right mind to have this discussion now, but it has to happen."

Chris turned to look at Taylor and nodded. "Sure thing. Good night."

While walking back to his room, Chris began to wonder how Taylor managed to party so hard while earning high grades and breaking football records every season. "So, I just caught Taylor and his friend doing coke in the kitchen," he informed Bryan as he entered his bedroom.

"What?" Bryan asked, sitting up straight on the futon.

Chris shut his door behind him and nodded.

Bryan widened his brown eyes. "No way!"

Chris laughed and sat down on his bed. "Yeah, way. That's why they're going to win the beer pong tournament. I always wondered how he could drink so much and stay sober. He's probably been doing coke all night."

"Woah, dude. You *own* him."

Chris nodded. "Yup. He wants to talk about it tomorrow. He's mortified."

"Are you going to tell Marc and Jordan?"

Chris shrugged. "I don't know. It depends on what he says. Marc would be upset. Jordan's partied at Northeastern before, so I'm sure he already knows what Taylor does."

"That's crazy. Then that story we heard outside must be true."

"I figured. I overheard one of his friends talking about coke last year. Since then, I've assumed they're all into it. Taylor wasn't ever going to admit that to me."

"Well now he has no choice."

"Yeah. Right."

"I'm kind of shocked. I mean, Taylor's known as a role model," Bryan said. "He even came and spoke at my school. He was talking about how you have to be disciplined to succeed. He doesn't seem too disciplined now."

"Not at all. He's way more laid back than he used to be. He was always kind of like Marc—serious about everything. Even after he got arrested for streaking with the cheerleaders, I still looked up to him because I thought it was a fantastic senior prank. It sucks that he lost his eligibility to play for Notre Dame because of it though."

"That's why he didn't go to ND?"

"Yeah, guy. They rescinded their offer. Haven't you ever wondered why Taylor isn't playing on a top-ranked team? He's sick. He messed up bigtime."

"How did your family keep *that* out of the news?"

Chris shrugged. "People still know about it. So many kids have brought it up to me, saying Taylor's 'the man.' He's still idolized by everyone around here."

"Do you think he'll make it to the NFL?"

"Hopefully, he'll transfer to a school with more of an audience while he's still eligible to play. I think it's crazy that Jordan's the one who's going to be playing at ND. He's never taken football that seriously."

"It has to bother Taylor that Jordan signed with them."

Chris nodded. "Why do you think Taylor parties so hard now? Clearly, something's not right in his head."

"Well, let me know how your talk goes," Bryan said with a short laugh before rolling over on the futon. "I'm passing out."

While trying to fall asleep a few moments later, Chris imagined what his parents would say if they knew he had caught Taylor with cocaine. He wondered if they would even care. He was thankful his younger sister Katie was spending the weekend with Taylor's parents and had not been exposed to the debauchery of that evening.

Despite how much fun Chris had that night, a part of him wondered if he was becoming a bad influence on his friends. He felt responsible for Chantal and Jon's argument earlier that evening. Chantal meant the world to Jon, and Chris realized she could break up with him over what had happened. Although he was almost certain Jon would wait a long time before drinking again, Chris resolved not to pressure him anymore. Obviously, the alcohol and weed had worn off because he was thinking quite clearly and feeling rather guilty.

CHAPTER 25

ATHY AWOKE THE NEXT morning to find herself alone in Lisa's queen-sized canopy bed. She glanced at the clock on the nearby nightstand: 8:33A.M. *How early does this girl get up?*

The girls had stayed up long past midnight, talking about everything from Chris's party to Lisa's home-life. Cathy had learned that Lisa's mother had abandoned her family ten years prior, leaving her father alone to raise Lisa and her brothers: JC and Joe. JC was soon to graduate from Babson College, and Joe was a junior at BU. Both boys intended to pursue law degrees and one day work at their father's well-established law firm.

"Because my brothers are so much older than me, I've always assumed I was a mistake-baby," Lisa had admitted before falling asleep. "Sometimes I think I'm the reason why my mother left—like she couldn't bear the thought of raising another child."

Cathy had felt extremely awkward while Lisa shared her story. She had never known Lisa to talk openly about her feelings, and she honestly had no idea what to say in return. Cathy was blessed to have parents who prioritized their children over everything. She could not begin to empathize with Lisa, but she felt overwhelmed with sympathy for her entire family. Cathy was in awe that the girl whom everyone envied for her beauty and popularity carried so much internal pain. She was happy that Lisa had confided in her, realizing that Lisa might need a friend just as much as she did.

"Hey! You're up!" Lisa exclaimed as she entered her bedroom in pajamas.

"I couldn't sleep, so I went downstairs and had coffee with my dad."

"You drink coffee?" Cathy asked in surprise.

"Yeah, my dad lets me drink it with him on the weekends. He's a workaholic, so coffee is his best friend. Are you hungry? We can make breakfast."

"I should call my mom and see what time she's picking me up. I don't know if she's coming before or after church."

"Do you think Jon will go to church?" Lisa asked and smiled with amusement. "Oh my gosh. I can't wait to see how this all plays out. I'm sure Chris will tell me everything that happened after we left. I'm so curious!"

"I doubt Jon will even be awake for church, and I'm sure he wants to avoid Chantal. I'm so afraid she's going to get her heart broken," Cathy admitted.

Lisa sat down on her bed beside Cathy. "We both know Jon is no party-boy."

"Yeah, but he cares a lot about staying close with his friends."

"True."

"Chantal's afraid he's going to follow Chris's lead."

"Chris is not a bad kid," Lisa remarked. "I can't see him getting his friends into too much trouble."

"For the record, I think Chris is awesome. He's nice to everyone and super fun. I'm happy you guys are together, but I can see Tal's point."

"Well if Jon keeps slipping up, maybe she should give Andy another chance."

Cathy rolled her eyes.

"I know you hate him, but trust me, he really is a good kid. He would treat Chantal like a treasure."

"She is a treasure."

"You can't hate Andy for letting Chantal drink spiked punch if you don't hate me for it."

True. Cathy sighed.

"Andy doesn't drink or smoke, and he doesn't attend wild parties. He spends most of his time volunteering, playing hockey, and doing schoolwork. He told me he would go back to youth group with you guys, and I'm sure he would go to church. He would be really good for Chantal," Lisa pressed.

"You're not going to give up on this, are you?"

"Probably not. I have good intuition, and I think Andy's a better fit. Are you going to tell Chantal that Jon got drunk?"

Cathy shook her head. "That has to come from him. I don't want to get in the middle. I like Jon a lot, and I think they both could have handled things better last night."

***

An hour later while the girls were making pancakes in the kitchen, the Ankermans' house phone began ringing. Lisa's eyes widened with excitement as Chris's number appeared on the caller ID. "I knew you'd have stuff to tell me," she said as soon as she picked up the receiver. "Oh, shoot, sorry. Hi, Jon!"

Cathy raised her eyebrows in surprise. *I can't believe he's awake.*

"Yeah, she's still here. Hold on," Lisa said before passing the phone to Cathy.

Cathy's stomach dropped. *So much for not getting in the middle.* "What's up?" she asked, trying to sound relaxed.

"I need to know if you're going to tell Chantal about what happened last night. Did you already say something?"

"I haven't talked to her," Cathy replied.

"She'll kill me. It will be the end of us if she finds out what I did. Please do not tell her."

"You don't have to worry about me saying anything. I don't want to get in the middle, but honestly, what the heck is going on with you?"

Jon let out a heavy breath. "I let my anger get the best of me. That's the only explanation I can give. You know I'm against drinking."

"I know that, but do *you* know that?"

"I do. It was a momentary lapse of reason, and it's not going to happen again."

"I think you need to pray long and hard about spending time at Chris's house. You're not exactly being the positive influence you hoped to be."

Jon let out another heavy breath. "I know."

"If you do anything like this again, I'll tell Chantal about what happened last night," Cathy warned.

"Fine. Deal. Thank you for keeping this quiet."

"Why are you up so early? I thought you'd be hungover."

"I have to go to church if I want to make things right with Tal. My mom's picking me up soon."

"Good luck. I'm staying at Lisa's for the day, but maybe I'll see you later if you end up at my house."

"Yeah, we'll see. Thanks, Cathy. I owe you."

CHAPTER 26

BY 11:00 A.M., ALL guests had vacated Chris's house, leaving him alone in the kitchen, surrounded by party debris. Marc and Taylor were yet to stir, leading Chris to believe it had been a very late night. He decided to begin the clean-up job that was sure to take hours.

Moments later, Chris moved throughout his basement, putting empty cups and cans into a large trash bag. He wondered what Taylor was going to say to him. Chris assumed his cousin was dreading the conversation. In fact, he was probably wide awake in bed trying to decide how to handle the situation.

If Chris were to tell his aunt and uncle what he had witnessed, they would be devastated. Taylor was the "golden child" in their family. Even when he got caught streaking, his parents had blamed the cheerleaders. They seemed incapable of seeing that Taylor had a wild streak within him. Instead, they wrote Jordan off as their "wild child" and as a result expected much less from him. All their hopes seemed to lie in Taylor, even though Jordan and Marc were exceptional students and athletes.

If Chris were to out Taylor to his aunt and uncle or to his parents, there was a decent chance they would no longer allow him to housesit. That would dash Chris's hopes of throwing the best parties in Montgomery. He wanted to be the source of fun for his friends, and he liked bringing people together under his roof. Therefore, ratting on Taylor was out of the question.

Chris continued to clean the basement until he heard footsteps on the stairs. A few seconds later, Marc appeared with a vacuum in his hand. He looked surprised to see Chris. "How long have you been cleaning?"

Chris shrugged.

"Taylor should be the one doing this," Marc muttered.

"I think he's going to be in bed for quite a while," Chris commented dryly.

"He told me what happened."

Chris let out a heavy breath. "Yeah, we have an awkward conversation in our future."

"I don't know why he's messing with drugs. He knows addiction runs in our family, and he remembers what my dad was like when he used to drink," Marc rambled.

Chris shrugged. "Beats me."

"You have to be careful, too. It's easier than you think to get addicted to stuff."

Chris knew Marc was right, but he did not plan on doing any single drug enough to become addicted. He just wanted to try what he saw other people enjoying. "I'm just experimenting."

"Yeah, well, keep a close watch on Taylor because, in his mind, he's just experimenting, too."

"Aren't you curious at all?" Chris asked. "Have you tried *anything*?"

Marc shook his head. "Not really. I've never smoked anything, and I've never been drunk," Marc replied. "I drank with Jordan and Taylor a few times this year, but that's it."

"Damn. I've done worse stuff than you," Chris stated and widened his eyes. "I figured you had at least been drunk before. You're the true 'golden child' in our family."

Marc smirked. "Maybe if I break one of Taylor's football records, my parents will see that."

"At least they don't think you're a black sheep."

"Jordan *is* a black sheep."

"No, c'mon, he's not."

"Um, he tried to date-rape my friend, and he bought you hard liquor. I'm pretty sure he's the one who let you smoke pot two weeks ago. Taylor was too drunk to remember the night, so Jordan said Taylor let you do it, but I know he would never do that. T never smoked weed in high school, let alone middle school. Jordan's been smoking weed for years. I don't even think he stops during football season. I'm not naïve, Chris."

Chris laughed. "Fine. Taylor never let me smoke, but Jordan didn't try to rape Michelle."

"Really?" Marc asked sarcastically and raised his eyebrows. "You were in the room with me when we found her topless and passed out."

"Jordan told me she puked all over her shirt, so he asked her to take it off before getting into my bed. I appreciate that."

"She was only puking because he drugged her. Michelle doesn't drink. He made her sick."

"I have a hard time believing that," Chris retorted. He remembered seeing Michelle and Jordan together at the party before she became ill, and it was clear that they were both into each other. Chris assumed this bothered Marc because he had been in love with Michelle since they dated in middle school. Chris found it bewildering that Marc would rather believe Jordan was capable of drugging someone than believe Michelle actually liked his brother.

"Michelle avoids Jordan for a reason," Marc stated flatly.

"Well maybe it's for a different reason than you think."

"Look, I know you love Jordan, but he's done a lot of bad things. The fact that he's going to Notre Dame next year is a miracle. I honestly doubt he'll last a semester without getting kicked out."

"I guess we'll just have to see," Chris commented. Personally, he believed Jordan got a bad rap because of his fun-loving personality. He seemed to float through life without a care in the world, and more serious people—like Marc and Taylor—judged him for it.

The sound of the basement door creaking open drew Chris's attention away from his thoughts. He assumed the footsteps heading his way belonged to Taylor, and his stomach began to flutter. A few seconds later, Taylor entered the room, wearing a Patriots hat, a gray hooded sweatshirt, and navy-blue sweatpants. He had dark circles around his eyes, and he looked exhausted. He shot his eyes from Chris to Marc and let out a heavy breath. "Go upstairs, you two," he said. "This is my mess to clean."

The way Marc said "fine" and immediately dropped the vacuum to the floor led Chris to believe he was quite angry with his brother.

"Chris, go relax," Taylor insisted. "We'll talk in a bit. I have to get this place cleaned up before your parents get home."

"All right," Chris agreed in a somber tone. He could tell by the expression on Taylor's face that he felt humiliated.

As Chris passed by him on the way to the stairs, Taylor put his hand on Chris's shoulder. "I'm sorry," he said in a tone filled with conviction.

Chris dropped his eyes to the floor and walked past his cousin. "I'll be in my room when you're ready to talk," he said before walking up the stairs.

CHAPTER 27

TWO HOURS LATER, CHRIS was lying on his bed, watching the Bruins matinee, when he heard Taylor knock on his bedroom door. "Come in," he called.

Taylor opened the door and walked over to Chris's futon with his head down. "I messed up last night," he said after a few seconds, "in more ways than one."

Chris muted the television and turned to face his cousin.

Taylor sighed. "For one, I never should have allowed my friends to bring cocaine into your house."

Chris nodded.

"And two, I shouldn't have let my obsession with winning the tournament move me to do coke. The three-hundred-dollar prize was not worth exposing you to it. I don't blame you for being upset about everything. Marc is pissed, and he has every right to be. I got too caught up in the competition to weigh out the pros and cons. I'm competitive to a fault."

"Do you do coke a lot?" Chris asked, aware that his cousin had not exactly said he was wrong for using the drug in general.

Taylor shook his head. "Just when I overdo it with drinking and need to sober up. Some of my friends are big into it, so it's always around. I don't blame you if you don't believe me, but it's really not something I do. I was being honest when I said I usually stick to beer."

"What about other stuff?" Chris asked.

Taylor sighed. "I've never smoked a cigarette, and I rarely smoke weed.

You should stay away from both. I've done a lot of molly. My friends and I were into raves and clubs for a couple of years. Honestly, I hated the way it left me dehydrated for days at a time. I stopped doing it last year, and I've always stayed away from drugs during football season."

"What about prescription stuff?" Chris pressed.

Taylor shook his head. "No. I don't mess with that. Addiction runs in our family and pills can take you down a scary road."

Chris could tell that Taylor was being honest with him, and he appreciated it.

"I understand if you need to tell your parents," Taylor stated. "I'm prepared to deal with the consequences."

Chris shook his head and let out a short laugh. "No way. I want you to still be able to housesit."

Taylor smiled. "Well, I appreciate that. I have to leave in a few minutes to pick your parents up at the airport. Do you want to come?"

"No, I want to watch the game," Chris replied—he had no desire to see his parents.

"All right, well, is there anything else you want to talk about?"

"You didn't let me try weed a couple of weeks ago," Chris admitted. "Jordan did." He could tell Taylor felt horrible about everything, so he figured knowing the truth about his marijuana use would make Taylor feel a little better.

"That's a relief," Taylor said. "I should have known Jordan was pranking me."

"Marc thinks Jordan will get kicked out of Notre Dame. Do you think he's really that messed up?"

Taylor shook his head. "He'll buckle down when he needs to. Jordan's carefree, *but* he's extremely competitive on the field. I think he'll do just fine."

"I hope so," Chris said. "Are you going to try to transfer next year?"

Taylor shrugged. "Maybe. I have to reach out to some coaches and see if anyone needs a QB. I want to be on a starting roster, and most teams already have their starting quarterbacks. I waited too long to transfer. I don't have an extra year of eligibility to just ride the bench."

"That sucks."

"Yeah, another mistake. My coach loves me, so I'm hoping he'll put in a good word for me with some scouts. The NFL has drafted some players from Northeastern but not many. We'll just have to see what happens."

"I hope I get a scholarship to college like you and Jordan," Chris commented.

"Then stay away from drugs," Taylor insisted. "There's no way I would have gotten the offers I did if I had partied in high school. I was as straightedge as Marc. Coaches care a lot about character."

"I'll keep that in mind," Chris said, knowing Taylor was saying what needed to be said. His recent use of illicit drugs, however, gave his warning much less merit.

CHAPTER 28

***

One Month Later

AFTER FINISHING HIS ALGEBRA homework, Jason Davids looked at the clock: 10:37 P.M. Deciding it was too late to call his best friend Chris's house, he went onto Facebook to send him a private message. Jason scrolled through Chris's posts of the many parties he had missed while skiing with his family every weekend during ski season. It seemed like his friends had all grown closer without him, and that bothered him a lot. Moreover, they were spending a lot of time with girls—cute girls—and Jason hated being left out of the fun. Ski season was almost over, so this would be his last weekend at Sugarloaf for a while—thank God.

Hey dude. Are you having a party next weekend? I'll be around. Call my cell if you're still up. Miss you, bro, Jason typed into his phone and hit send. He went back to Chris's profile and looked at his pictures. *Lisa is so hot,* he thought as he locked his blue eyes on a picture of Chris's girlfriend. *Good job, buddy.* As he clicked from one photo to the next, he noticed that Chantal had finally gotten her twin sister Cathy to hang out with them. *She's cute.*

Jason liked Chantal a lot and thought she was perfect for her boyfriend Jon Anderson because of their shared faith. Jon and Jason had been friends since Jon first moved to Montgomery in third grade. Despite how often Jason teased Jon for attending church and youth group, Jason thought it was good for him—Jon's relationship with Chantal proved that much. Jason began to wonder if Cathy was bubbly and outgoing like her twin or if she was more reserved. The fact that it had taken her so long to begin hanging out with their group of friends led Jason to assume the latter.

Jason's middle school, St. Timothy's, was an all-boys school, so Jason had more of an itch than any of his friends to spend time with girls. At every party he attended over the past year, he hooked up with someone. The problem was that he liked girls too much to stay interested in just one. Random girls were fine for hookups, but Jason knew he could not do that to Chantal's sister, despite how attractive she was. If she had become a part of his inner circle, then he could not cross that line even if the opportunity presented itself.

Facebook disappeared on his iPhone as a call from Chris appeared on the screen. "What's up, guy?" Jason called as he flopped down on his bed.

"You're at Sugarloaf, right?"

"Yup. Last weekend of the season."

"Well, you're not missing anything this weekend because my parents are home from London. Taylor and Jordan are babysitting next weekend, so a party will be in order."

"Excellent."

"Are you actually going to drink if they let us?"

"Probably not," Jason replied. "I'm sure Matt and Luke will be there with Marc, and they would kill me."

"Marc probably won't come because he's mad at Jordan, so I don't know if your brothers will be here—maybe Matt if everyone else on the football team comes."

"Yeah, well, Matt would tear me apart if I took a sip of beer, so you should probably look for another drinking buddy," Jason stated with a short laugh.

"Will do. You can invite a girl if you want. Are you still talking to Kristen?" Chris asked, referring to the girl Jason had lost his virginity to earlier in the schoolyear.

"No," Jason replied. "I was never around, so she moved on to some kid in her grade. It's for the best. The spark between us burned out fast."

"I think you'll like Chantal's sister."

"Ha. I was actually just looking at her picture on Facebook. She's hot."

"Lisa and Cathy are pretty much inseparable now, so we've hung out a lot lately. She's very witty."

"Sounds like Lisa."

"Yeah. They're definitely meant to be best friends."

"Is she super Christian like Chantal?"

"She is, but you wouldn't know unless you asked her about it," Chris replied. "She's hard to get to know."

Jason laughed. "Also like Lisa. You're basically describing your girlfriend to me."

"Right."

"I can't hook up with Chantal's sister," Jason stated. "That would make things awkward for everyone."

"I honestly don't even think she'd hook up with you," Chris said, taking Jason by surprise.

"Really?"

"Yeah. She's not flirty at all. I just think if you guys got to know each other, you'd like each other."

"I don't want a girlfriend," Jason stated flatly, "but I'll keep that in mind." He wondered what he would have to do to get Cathy to like him; he loved a challenge.

CHAPTER 29

***

One Week Later

"I LOOK SO WEIRD WITH makeup on," Cathy said as she stared at her reflection in Lisa's full-length mirror. "I'm going to wipe this eyeshadow off."

"Leave it! You look beautiful!" Lisa cried in protest.

"But I feel weird."

"But you look great."

Cathy sighed. "Fine."

"Everything about you looks perfect. I love your hair scrunched like that, and you look fantastic in my dress," Lisa remarked. She certainly had a way of making Cathy feel comfortable.

"If you say so," Cathy complied.

"This is going to be the biggest party Chris has ever hosted," Lisa said. "Taylor and Jordan invited a whole slew of people over, and they let Chris invite everyone he wanted."

"Should be fun," Cathy remarked, again peering at her reflection. Lisa and Cathy were thankfully both size threes, so Lisa's black cocktail dress fit her perfectly. Lisa was also dressed up, wearing a sparkly red dress and black wedge heels. Cathy knew their attire would draw a lot of attention their way, and she wasn't quite sure how she felt about that.

CHAPTER 30

Jason's father dropped him off at Chris's house around seven o'clock that evening, a half hour before the older kids were due to arrive. He was dressed in his usual, preppy attire: a blue, short-sleeved, striped dress-shirt, loose khaki pants, and brown leather shoes. When he had spiked his black hair, Cathy had been on his mind. For some reason, he wanted to look perfect for her. Neither Matt nor Luke was attending the party, so Jason would have the freedom to let loose if he so pleased. He wasn't sure that he wanted to exploit that liberty, though, because he wanted to be on top of his game.

When Chris answered the door, Jason could tell he had been pre-gaming. His eyes were glassy, and he had a childish grin on his face. "JD!" he exclaimed and slapped hands with Jason. "Good to see you, buddy."

Jason let out a short laugh. "Are you buzzed or baked?"

"A little bit of both," Chris replied and shut the door behind him.

"What's up, Jon?" Jason greeted his friend sitting on the couch with a slight nod.

"Good to see you, guy," Jon replied.

"Jon just took two shots of Fireball with me upstairs," Chris whispered to Jason. "He's already buzzed."

"What?!" Jason cried as an amused smile spread across his face. "Jonny-boy, you drink now?"

"No, but tonight yes," Jon replied.

Jason laughed. "I've missed a lot, I guess."

"You have," Chris agreed.

A few moments later, Chris's doorbell rang. "That's probably Lisa," he said as he jumped off the couch. He hustled to the door and swung it open. "Hey, gorgeous!" he exclaimed and stepped aside to let Lisa and Cathy into his house.

Jason's eyes widened as he glanced toward the doorway. Both girls were absolutely stunning. Lisa looked even prettier than Jason had remembered, and Cathy looked just as beautiful as her. He had never seen a picture of Cathy dressed up, so the sight of her nearly took his breath away. For the first time in a long time, he felt nervous.

◑   ◑   ◑

As Cathy stepped past Chris into his living room, she did a double take. She had expected to see Bryan and Jon on the couch, but the kid she saw with Jon was not Bryan; he was somehow even cuter than Bryan. She tore her eyes off him and smiled at Chris. "Thanks so much for having us over," she said cheerfully, attempting to regain her composure.

"Thanks for coming!" Chris cried and closed the door behind them. "You guys look great!"

Cathy could tell by the pitch of his voice that Chris had already begun drinking. "Thanks," she said.

"Hi, guys!" Lisa exclaimed, waving at the other two boys.

"What's up, Lisa?" the gorgeous kid with black hair and blue eyes said as he rose from the couch. He walked over to Lisa and gave her a hug. "I haven't seen you in months! I can't believe you're still dating this loser," he teased and nodded toward Chris.

Lisa laughed. "I've missed you, Jay!"

Cathy widened her eyes. *Jason!* She had completely given up on meeting him. Cocking her head to the side, she smiled. *So, you're the witty, taunting player I've heard so much about.*

"And who's this?" Jason asked Lisa and locked his aquamarine eyes on Cathy.

"I'm Cathy," she blurted out before Lisa could introduce them.

"Jason," he stated and extended his right hand toward her. When they shook hands, Cathy's stomach fluttered, and she hoped to God she wasn't blushing.

"Hey, girls," Jon greeted them as he appeared between Jason and Chris.

Cathy leaned in to hug him. "Is everything, okay?" she asked quietly.

"Yeah, why wouldn't it be?" Jon answered once she freed him from her embrace.

Cathy shrugged. "You just look a little down; that's all."

"I'm fine."

Cathy squinted her eyes in thought. *You and Chantal must have had another fight.* She hated the noticeable distance that was expanding between Jon and her sister. The worst part was seeing them both upset so often.

"Can I get you girls a drink?" Chris offered.

"What do you have?" Lisa asked with a mischievous sparkle in her green eyes.

"Oh, you just wait," Chris said with a laugh. "Taylor's not letting us drink, but Jordan came to the rescue again. Not a bottle, though, because he doesn't want to get caught hooking me up this time, but he bought me some nips of Fireball—strong stuff. I saved one for you."

"Thank you," Lisa said in a flirty tone. "I'll take a water for now."

"Cathy?" Chris called.

"Yeah, water's great," Cathy replied distractedly. Jason was standing to her left, and he appeared to be checking her out. However, he was a flirt and a player by reputation, and she wanted nothing to do with someone like that—even though butterflies were still fluttering around in her stomach.

CHAPTER 31

CHANTAL ARRIVED AT CHRIS's house with Alyssa around eight o'clock when the party was in full swing. Cathy saw them enter the living room, and she could tell her sister was overwhelmed by the scene. Even so, she looked beautiful with her auburn hair flowing perfectly straight down her back. She was wearing a black skirt, a sparkly silver top, and black flats. Alyssa was also dressed to impress in a tight white dress and bright red heels. Her long, dirty-blonde hair was curled at the ends, and her makeup looked like it had been professionally applied. Alyssa was the fashion diva of their group—no doubt.

Cathy stood up from the chair she had been sitting in and hustled over to Alyssa and Chantal. "Hi! I'm so glad you're here!" she exclaimed and threw her arms around her sister, hoping to make her feel more comfortable. Chantal hugged her back tightly. Cathy pulled free from Chantal and quickly embraced Alyssa before turning back toward her sister. "What's up?"

"Nothing. Just happy to be here," Chantal replied with a forced smile.

Cathy cocked her head to the side. "You know I know you better than that."

Chantal rolled her green eyes. "Jon and I got in another fight—literally over nothing."

"Are you guys okay now?" Cathy inquired, glancing over at Jon who was sitting with Jason and Chris on the couch.

Chantal shrugged.

"He's kind of being a jerk," Alyssa said and nodded toward him. "Hopefully, he snaps out of it." Alyssa and Jon were as close as siblings, so Cathy was surprised to hear Alyssa say anything negative about him.

Chantal stepped past Cathy and walked over towards Jon. He rose from his seat when he noticed her. Cathy watched as they awkwardly embraced each other. For once, Jon did not look happy to see her. "What happened?" Cathy whispered to Alyssa.

"He told her she didn't have to come tonight," Alyssa replied.

"What?"

"Yeah, like, out of nowhere, he just said it would be okay if she stayed home. Usually, he begs her to come here."

"Was he just trying to give her an out?"

Alyssa shrugged. "She took it personally, as though he didn't want her here."

Cathy crossed her arms. "I'd like to believe he said it because of how upset she got with him at Chris's party last month, but I think it might be more than that."

Alyssa nodded. "He's being really weird—and not just toward her."

"Well, let's go over there and see how she is," Cathy said. She was baffled: Jon had been smitten over Chantal for the past six months. His behavior of late was erratic and senseless.

"Hi, Lyss," Jon greeted Alyssa as soon as the girls reached him. He gave her a hug and a much warmer smile than he had given Chantal.

"Hi, buddy," she said and embraced him tightly. Jon waited an abnormally long amount of time before letting go of Alyssa, which caused Chantal to drop her eyes to the floor. Despite the thunderous party erupting around them, there was perceivable tension in the air surrounding them. Cathy hoped Chris would come up with a way to lighten the mood quickly.

"Guys, I think we should go outside and play Manhunt," Jason suddenly proposed.

Cathy let out a short laugh. "What?"

"It's so nice out tonight! It's, like, sixty degrees. Chris has the perfect backyard for it," Jason stated enthusiastically. "Let's do it."

Chris laughed. "I had other ideas in mind, but that's just as good as any."

"We're in dresses," Alyssa protested. "We can't go play in the dirt."

"That's a good point," Lisa agreed.

"You girls could borrow some of my sister's clothes," Chris offered.

"Why don't we play Manhunt another night this week?" Cathy suggested. "I like the idea."

Jason smiled. "Works for me."

"So, want to get a card game going?" Chris asked.

"What about Catan?" Jason suggested in a bright-eyed manner. "Oh, that game's the best!"

"If you want to play, feel free," Chris said. "It requires more thinking than I feel like doing, but anyone who wants to play, go for it."

"Do you want to play?" Jason asked as he turned toward Cathy and tapped her arm.

"I'm guessing Catan is a strategy game?" she assumed.

Jason smiled and nodded. "It's fantastic."

Cathy shrugged. "I'm up for it."

"Alyssa? Chantal?" Jason asked, raising his eyebrows.

"Yeah, sure," Chantal replied. "Sounds fun."

"Sounds better than Manhunt in a white dress!" Alyssa cried.

"I'll hang out with Chris," Lisa said and wrapped her arms around her boyfriend.

Jon looked somewhat torn.

"It's a four-player game, but you and Chantal can be a team if you want to play, Jon," Jason said.

Jon shook his head. "No, it's okay. I don't really feel like thinking much tonight either. You guys have fun. I'll hang out with Chris and Lisa. Bryan will be showing up soon, too."

Cathy watched as Chantal's face fell. It seemed as though Jon was trying to avoid her, but Cathy could not even begin to speculate why he would act that way.

CHAPTER 32

AFTER JASON LED CATHY, Chantal, and Alyssa upstairs to play Catan in the Dunkins' study, Chris brought Lisa and Jon up to his bedroom. "I have six nips of Fireball left," he said as he stacked the bottles side-by-side on his bureau. "Two each?"

Lisa darted her green eyes at Jon with a look of utter shock. "You're going to drink?" she asked.

"Just give me one," Jon said and held out his hand.

"Whatever you want," Chris responded and passed Jon a bottle. "Lisa?"

Lisa widened her eyes and sent Chris a questioning glance. He assumed she was a bit perplexed by Jon's behavior. "Um, yeah, okay," she stammered.

Chris took the cap off and handed the nip to Lisa. He held up his own and said, "Cheers to Jay working his magic and getting Cathy's number by the end of the night."

"Ha! That's a good one," Lisa remarked.

"Cheers," Jon said and held up his drink. They clinked their bottles together and threw back the fiery shots.

"It burns!" Lisa exclaimed and began coughing.

"Sorry. I should have warned you," Chris apologized. "I wish Taylor would just let us drink from the keg."

"This stuff is too strong," Jon stated. He was three shots deep without a tolerance, and Chris could tell he was already buzzed. He thought Jon was making a huge mistake.

"We should go back downstairs in case Leslie and Katherine arrive," Lisa suggested.

"Good thinking," Chris said and led Lisa and Jon out of his room before Jon could consider taking another shot. He could hear Jason laughing in the nearby study and assumed he was laying his charm on Cathy. "We can hang out in the kitchen with Jordan and his friends," he said while walking downstairs. "Taylor and his crew took over the basement."

In Chris's large kitchen, beer pong, flip cup, and a few other drinking games were taking place. The room was filled with juniors and seniors from Montgomery Lake High, who all extolled Jordan as their mighty leader. He was sitting at the granite-topped island, shuffling a deck of cards. Of course, there were pretty girls on either side of him.

"What up, Little D?" Jordan called as Chris approached him.

"Just scoping out the scene."

"Good deal. Where are the rest of your friends?"

"Some are playing a game upstairs; others are still on their way," Chris replied.

"Cool. You all set with drinks?"

"As set as I'm allowed to be," Chris retorted.

Jordan laughed. "I'm going to roll a blunt in a few minutes. Stay close."

Chris's eyes lit up for a second until he realized that news probably disturbed Lisa. She had made it clear to him that she didn't like him smoking pot. He turned away from Jordan to look at her. She raised one eyebrow at him, as if to say, *don't even think about it.* "We'll be back," Chris said and tapped the countertop. "C'mon guys. Let's go in the living room."

Leslie, Katherine, and Bryan all arrived within the following ten minutes and so did Lisa's friends from Sterling: Bobby Ryan, Adam Case, and Andy Rosetti. Chris had forgotten to warn Jon that Lisa had invited Andy, and the look on Jon's face was indescribable when Andy entered the room.

"Andy! Thank you so much for coming!" Lisa exclaimed, rushing off to hug her best friend, who was dressed nicely in a black Polo shirt and khakis. His black hair was spiked up, and Chris assumed he had dressed up for Chantal.

Andy flashed a wide smile at Lisa. "Anything for you. Hi, Chris," he said and leaned forward to shake Chris's hand. "Thanks for the invite."

"No problem. What's up, guys?" Chris greeted Adam and Bobby while Jon shot daggers at him.

"Can I talk to you for a second?" Jon interrupted Chris.

"Yeah, sure, guy," Chris replied and stepped off to the side.

"What the heck?!" Jon exclaimed.

Chris widened his eyes. "I'm sorry! I forgot he was coming. He usually doesn't show up. I think Lisa really pushed him to come tonight."

Jon scowled. "Take me to your room. I want another shot."

Chris sighed. "Jon, c'mon. You have to chill. Your girlfriend is upstairs. She's going to lose it on you. Do you really want that to happen in front of Andy?"

Jon hung his head. "No."

"Let's just go into another room and calm down," Chris said, hoping he could somehow prevent drama from invading his party.

"Fine," Jon huffed.

"Hey, Lis, we'll be right back," Chris called to her before leaving the room. He hoped she could read his eyes and decipher that he was trying to put space between Jon and Andy. She smiled and gave him a thumbs up sign.

"I don't want Chantal and Andy to talk," Jon said to Chris as they stood by the refrigerator a moment later.

"Then maybe you should start paying attention to her."

"I need some space, but I don't want to lose her. I don't think I've ever felt this confused," Jon admitted.

"No more alcohol for you, guy," Chris stated, lowering his eyebrows. This was the least fun party he had ever hosted, and he wanted to change that as quickly as possible.

"Little D!" Jordan called to Chris from the kitchen's island. "Come here."

Chris nodded for Jon to follow him over to where Jordan was sitting with his friends. Sure enough, Jordan had rolled the aforementioned blunt and was expecting Chris to smoke with him. "This is for everyone in the kitchen, so just take one hit and pass it on," Jordan said while handing the blunt to Chris.

Chris had never smoked a blunt before and felt slightly intimidated by its size. For that reason, he only took a small hit, hoping of course that Lisa was nowhere in sight.

"Let me try that," Jon said.

"No!" Chris exclaimed and widened his eyes. "You're not thinking straight."

"Chris, you can't be a hypocrite like that," Jordan remarked playfully. "Who are you? Taylor?"

At that point, Chris felt sick to his stomach. He was watching one of his best friends make a series of terrible decisions, and he felt somewhat responsible. Chris was not an angry person, so he could not comprehend why

Jon's wrath was moving him to act so out of character.

Jordan snatched the blunt out of Chris's hand and passed it to Jon. "Just hit it."

Watching Jon smoke weed for the first time completely killed Chris's buzz. He knew Jon would be filled with regret the next day, and he hated watching him sabotage his relationship with Chantal. She was sure to come downstairs and check on him soon. To Chris, it seemed as though Jon was purposely trying to hurt her.

CHAPTER 33

"YOU JUST BLOCKED MY road!" Jason exclaimed, dropping his jaw and widening his blue eyes. "I had plans for that intersection!"

Cathy laughed. "Sorry—not sorry. I'm building on that spot, and I have the resources to do it." Catan involved dice, and Cathy enjoyed figuring out the odds of numbers being rolled to best position her real estate. Jason had been right: the game was extremely entertaining; it was like Risk and Monopoly combined but more fun than both. Cathy typically dominated strategy games when she played with her family, but Jason was giving her quite a challenge.

Chantal usually enjoyed planning and creating things, so Cathy had assumed she would be good at Catan as well. However, Chantal's mind was clearly on Jon and not the board before them. Alyssa was doing well, but she wasn't close to catching up with Jason. Cathy was the only one in reach of possibly beating him.

"Guys, do you mind if I take a quick break to go check on Jon?" Chantal asked, putting her cards face-down on the table.

"I'm surprised he hasn't come up here yet," Jason stated, eyeing Chantal with concern. "We'll keep the table warm for you."

"I'll go with you," Alyssa offered. "I want to see if Leslie and Katherine are here."

"Thanks," Chantal said and stood up to leave the room.

Cathy's heart began to pound at the realization she would soon be left alone with Jason. He was sitting to her left at the round, cherry table, and he appeared to be in deep thought.

"What's going on with your sister and Jon?" he asked a few seconds after Chantal and Alyssa left the room.

Cathy swallowed. "I don't know. Something's not right."

"So, he, like, drinks now?" Jason asked, raising his eyebrows.

"Oh, you heard about Chris's last party? Chantal doesn't know about that."

"Wait. What happened?"

"Oh. Well, wait. What are you talking about?"

Jason smirked. "Tell me first."

"They got in a fight, so Chantal left. Jon was upset, so he drank a bunch of rum and puked all night long."

Jason laughed. "You've got to be kidding me! I've missed so much. Before the winter, he berated Chris for drinking."

"Yeah, he's been acting weird lately. Did he berate you, too?" Cathy asked, wondering if Jason also drank.

Jason shook his head. "No. My older brothers are usually around, so I have an excuse not to drink. Chris knows they would kill me."

Cathy found his choice of words interesting. She didn't know if he meant he would drink if his brothers allowed him to or if he was glad that he had an excuse not to drink. Realizing that Jason had been purposely ambiguous, Cathy wondered if he was trying to impress her. "How old are your brothers?" she asked.

"Matt's a sophomore, and Luke's a freshman. They're friends with Chris's cousin Marc. They're out somewhere with him tonight."

"Oh, Marc's really nice," Cathy said.

Jason smiled. "Marc's like family to me. He practically lives at my house."

"He's hardly ever here. Do you think Jordan really tried to rape his friend?"

"Oh. I was here for that. It was quite a scene. Actually, I used to hang out with her sister Kristen, so I heard a lot about it after the fact."

"And?"

"Something made Michelle sick, but she claims Jordan didn't touch her."

"So she could have just had food poisoning or something?" Cathy wondered aloud.

"It's a mystery, but I don't think Jordan would ever force himself onto a girl."

Something suddenly dawned on Cathy. "So, wait. Backup. Why did you ask me if Jon drinks?" she wondered, realizing that if Jason did not know about the last party, then he must have heard about another incident.

"Because he drank with Chris tonight," Jason replied matter-of-factly.

Cathy widened her eyes. "He did?"

Jason nodded. "You couldn't tell he was buzzed?"

Cathy felt fury rising inside of her.

"You look pissed," Jason stated and raised his eyebrows at her.

Cathy dropped her jaw. "I'm going to kill him!" she cried and stood up from the table.

Jason looked slightly amused. "Can I watch?"

Cathy rolled her eyes. "C'mon." She fled the study and hustled down Chris's long second-floor hallway. Turning right down the bridal staircase, Cathy could feel Jason close behind her. With each step, the chant of the party grew louder. The stairs opened into the living room where many familiar faces were gathered. Cathy shot her eyes around the room, looking for Chantal or Jon.

"Chantal's over there," Jason said from behind Cathy, pointing toward her twin. Cathy squinted in disbelief that Chantal was talking to Andy Rosetti. *This just got a lot more interesting.* Cathy forgot that Lisa had persuaded him to attend the party. She had told him about Chantal and Jon's recent issues, insisting that he try to re-connect with her.

"Jon's going to lose it if he sees her talking to Andy," Cathy commented, "and Chantal's going to lose it if she finds out Jon drank tonight. They're a ticking time bomb."

"I don't see Jon or Chris. Let's check the kitchen," Jason suggested and tugged on Cathy's arm. He pulled her into the kitchen—a scene much rowdier than the living room. The party was livelier than the last one, thanks to Jordan's attendance.

Peering past the beer pong and flip cup tables, Cathy spotted Chris and Jon standing by the sink. "There they are," she said to Jason and pointed through the crowd.

"Let's go," Jason said and latched onto her hand to pull her through the sea of high school kids. Cathy's heart fluttered; she had never before allowed a boy to hold her hand.

"JD!" Chris exclaimed as soon as he noticed Jason and Cathy approaching them. "What's up, guy? You win already?"

Jason laughed. "I wish. The game is on hold for a bit."

Jon darted his eyes from Jason to Cathy and then down to their linked hands.

Cathy uncomfortably pulled her hand from Jason's grip and crossed her arms. "Jon, can I talk to you?" she asked, locking her eyes on him.

Jon dropped his brown eyes to the floor.

"Jay, come with me to check on Lisa," Chris said and nodded toward the hallway.

"She's in the living room. I'll meet you there in a second," Jason replied, clearly wanting to hear Cathy and Jon's exchange.

As Chris walked away from them, Cathy stepped closer to Jon. "What the heck is going on with you?" she asked, crouching down to try to make eye contact with him. He would not even look at her. "Look at me!" she demanded.

"I don't want to talk about Chantal right now," Jon replied, refusing to meet her eyes.

"Fine. Then let's talk about how you promised me you wouldn't drink again."

Jon sighed.

"I agreed not to tell my sister because you promised it would not happen again."

Jon looked up at her, and she realized his eyes were glassy.

"Sorry, guys, but I have to get out of here," Jon replied and immediately pushed past them.

CHAPTER 34

CHRIS WAS STANDING WITH Lisa, Chantal, and Andy when he noticed Jon enter the living room. "Chantal, I think Jon wants to talk to you," he said and nodded toward him, hoping to direct her attention away from Andy before Jon set his eyes on her.

Chantal turned around to locate her boyfriend. "I'll be back," she said and hustled across the room. Chris watched as she approached Jon and leaned in to hug him. There was a good chance she would detect that he was buzzed, and Chris could see a problem on the horizon.

Jon pulled free from Chantal's embrace and dropped his eyes to the floor. "I think I need to go home," he said. "I'm just not in the mood for this."

"What's going on?" Chantal asked and placed her hand on his arm. "Something feels off between us. I've never seen you act like this."

Jon looked up at her and hated the sadness he saw in her eyes. The guilt he felt for keeping his drunken incident from her had been eating away at him for weeks. Every time he looked at her, he felt bad for being dishonest, and that was why he was pushing her away. The only reason he had agreed to drink that night was because he thought it would numb the guilt he felt and make him more relaxed around her. After three shots, however, his guilt had only intensified. Nothing was going to make him feel better until he came clean.

He assumed telling Chantal the truth about Chris's last party would upset her. That was not something he wanted to have happen in the middle of the party, especially not with Andy in attendance. "Why don't we go upstairs and talk," he suggested and took her hand.

"I would like that," Chantal replied and allowed Jon to lead her upstairs to the study.

Cathy and Jason made their way through the living room to where Chris, Lisa, Alyssa, Bryan, and Andy were gathered. "Where's my sister?" Cathy asked as she approached the group.

"She went upstairs with Jon," Chris replied.

That sounded bad, Cathy thought.

"To talk!" Chris added. "No hooking up going on there."

"What's Jon's problem?" Cathy questioned him.

"Dude, was he high?" Jason asked from beside Cathy.

Chris smiled and laughed awkwardly. "He may or may not have taken a hit off a blunt Jordan passed around the kitchen."

Cathy widened her eyes.

"Did you smoke, too?" Lisa asked, tapping Chris on the shoulder.

"Don't hate me," Chris replied and smiled at his girlfriend.

Lisa crossed her arms and shook her head.

"I need to find Chantal," Cathy said.

"She's going to be really upset," Alyssa remarked and crossed her arms. "We'll probably be leaving. She's sleeping over my house tonight."

"Looks like we'll have to finish Catan another time," Jason said to Cathy and nudged her playfully in the side.

His flirting lightened her mood. "I think a rematch is in order," Cathy responded and nudged him back. Although she knew Jason was a "player" and most likely just trying to get in her pants, she enjoyed the attention he was paying her. He was cute, smart, funny, and sober: all very appealing attributes. She realized, however, that she needed to guard her heart. She could not let Jason, or anyone, know she was interested in him until he made it evident that he liked her. Jason clearly liked a challenge, and if they were ever going to be together, he would need to feel as though he had "won" her.

"So, are we just going to stand around and wait for the disaster that is Jon and Chantal to erupt?" Jason inquired. "Or can we go do something?"

"No Manhunt," Alyssa stated flatly.

Jason laughed. "What about a game of spoons in the dining room?"

"I like it!" Chris exclaimed.

"I'm up for that," Lisa replied.

Chris went to gather a deck of cards and spoons from the kitchen while Jason led everyone into the dining room and explained the rules of the game. Cathy liked how Jason seemed to always have a fun idea up his sleeve. She could tell that he liked to stay active, which only increased her attraction towards him.

The group was only a few minutes into the game when Chantal came rushing into the room. She appeared to have been crying, and Cathy wondered if she and Jon had broken up.

"What's up, Tal? Do you want to join the game?" Chris asked.

Chantal took a deep breath. "Actually, can I steal Alyssa and Cathy away for a second?"

Cathy put her cards on the bottom of the deck. "Count me out of this round," she said and hustled over to her sister. Alyssa did the same, and the girls accompanied Chantal into the hallway.

"You guys knew Jon got drunk last month?" Chantal questioned them, sounding hurt.

Alyssa let out a heavy breath.

"He made me promise not to tell you by promising me that he wouldn't drink again," Cathy explained. "I knew the truth would upset you, and I really liked you guys together, so I kept quiet; but after seeing his behavior tonight, I was planning to tell you everything. He broke his promise to me, and I don't really like you guys together anymore."

"He drank, again?" Alyssa asked, widening her eyes.

Chantal nodded. "He just told me everything upstairs. He's been taking shots of whiskey with Chris all night."

"I'm shocked," Alyssa stated. "Drinking is against his morals. His behavior makes no sense. Something's wrong with him."

"It's even worse," Chantal said. "He smoked weed with Chris. He's gone off the rails. I don't even know how to process this."

"Chris told us," Cathy said. "I'm just glad he admitted everything to you. Please don't be mad at us for not telling you."

"Jon should have told you the truth from the start, and we all felt it was his place to do that," Alyssa stated.

"I have lost so much respect for him," Chantal said. "I mean, a huge reason why I wanted to date him was because we had the same morals. If I wanted a party boy, I would have continued hanging out with Andy."

"According to Lisa, Andy doesn't party," Cathy said. "Not that I'm advocating for him by any means—you know how I feel about him—but evidently, losing you straightened him out."

"Whatever," Chantal commented carelessly. "I need to get out of here. I'm in no mood to socialize, and I don't want to be around Jon. I am so disgusted with him for so many reasons. Can I walk back to your house, Lyss? You don't have to leave."

"I'm not letting you walk to my house alone! We can leave. Jon's being a jerk," Alyssa stated. "I'm pissed at him for doing this to you."

"I'm supposed to sleep over Lisa's, but do you want me to come with you instead?" Cathy offered.

Chantal shook her head. "No. It's okay. I want you to enjoy the party. Lyss, are you sure you don't want to stay? I feel like I'm ruining your night."

"You're not ruining my night," Alyssa replied. "Jon's the one causing drama. Let's get our coats and go home."

Moments later, Chantal and Alyssa left Chris's house, and Cathy wondered if her sister would ever be back. Jon came downstairs a few moments later and joined everyone in the dining room. He sat next to Bryan and avoided eye contact with Cathy for the rest of the night.

CHAPTER 35

"**C**AN'T YOU JUST SLEEPOVER?" Chris asked, staring pleadingly into Lisa's green eyes hours later. Cathy and Lisa were due to leave the party in a half hour. All of their friends, except for Bryan and Jason, had already gone home. Cathy was relieved when Jon left shortly after Chantal.

"I would never be allowed to do that," Lisa replied. "Although it would be fun!"

"Can't you just say you're going to sleep at Cathy's house but stay here instead?" Chris proposed.

"Then what will Cathy do? She has to sleep at my house. Her mom isn't going to come pick her up *now*," Lisa stated matter-of-factly.

"She can stay over, too," Chris replied. "Have you seen the size of this house? We have two guest rooms upstairs, and I have a futon in my room."

Cathy's stomach fluttered.

Lisa turned to her. "My dad won't care if I say I'm sleeping at your house. What do you want to do?"

Cathy widened her eyes. She wished Lisa hadn't put her on the spot in front of everyone. She was having so much fun with Jason that she loved the idea of staying the night, but she hated the idea of lying to her parents. "I think my parents would ground me for a year if I stayed over."

"We don't want that," Jason commented and smiled at her. "We may have already lost one Kagelli twin tonight. We can't lose you both."

"I'll call my dad and ask if we can stay a little later," Lisa said to Chris.

"Okay?"

Chris smiled happily as Lisa ran off to call her father. Cathy assumed he wanted time to hook up with her: Lisa and Chris had been hooking up for months, doing things Cathy never thought people in seventh grade did. She had been shocked when Lisa told her about the physicality of their relationship. Although Lisa and Chris were both still virgins, they certainly enjoyed exploring each other's bodies. Cathy wondered if it was true that Jason had slept with an eighth grader. The possibility bothered her. She planned to wait until she was married to have sex, so if he did try to hook up with her, he was going to be quite disappointed.

Lisa returned a couple of moments later with a wide smile on her face. "My brother's home from college this weekend, and he said my dad is already in bed, so we can stay as late as we want."

"Nice!" Chris cried.

Cathy widened her eyes, wondering exactly how late Lisa would want to stay. "So, your brother will pick us up at any time?"

"Within reason," Lisa replied. "I wouldn't make him come out past two."

Cathy raised her eyebrows in surprise. Her parents never allowed her to stay out past ten o'clock, so abiding by Lisa's family's rules would be quite a treat.

"I like it," Chris said and threw his arms around Lisa. He picked her up off the ground and spun her around. "There's one more shot of Fireball left with your name on it, Lisa Ankerman. Upstairs we go."

"They'll be gone for a while," Jason commented as he watched Chris carry Lisa up the staircase.

"Yup. Much more than Fireball will be going on up there," Bryan laughed.

Cathy's stomach fluttered at the realization she had just been left with two of the hottest guys she knew.

"What do you guys want to do?" Jason asked, looking from Bryan to Cathy. The living room had been taken over by Jordan's high school friends, so they appeared a bit out of place.

"I wish Matt, Marc, or Luke were here," Bryan said. "I feel weird around Jordan and Taylor without them or Chris."

"Well, don't hold your breath for Marc to show up," Jason stated. "Why don't we lay claim to the big guest room before Taylor or Jordan takes it?"

"I bet someone already did," Bryan replied.

"It's worth checking out," Jason reasoned.

Cathy followed the boys through Chris's home. It was clear that Chris's parents made a lot of money during their frequent monthly travels. Their house was quite impressive with cutting-edge technology and high-end finishes in every room. Chris's bedroom was at the top of the stairs, and she heard him and Lisa laughing loudly when she passed by his room.

"They're having fun," Jason commented with a short laugh as he led Cathy and Bryan further down the hallway. The study, two guest rooms, two bathrooms, Chris's room, his sister Katie's room, and his parents' master suite comprised the second floor.

"Score!" Jason exclaimed as he stepped inside a bedroom and turned on the light. "I see no luggage. This one's all ours."

Cathy shot her eyes around the room: a king-sized sleigh bed with a large flat-screen TV across from it were the main focal points.

"Do you guys want to watch a movie?" Jason asked as he walked toward the TV. "They have everything on demand."

"Yeah, whatever," Bryan replied and sat down on the bed.

Cathy's stomach fluttered. There was no couch in the room, which meant she would be sharing a bed with Jason and Bryan if they watched a movie. Her heart pounded, and she felt a mixture of nerves and excitement.

"Cathy, I won't be surprised if you get through a whole movie before Lisa comes out of that room," Jason stated.

"Right?" Bryan laughed.

"I bet they have sex," Jason said and widened his blue eyes. "What do you think, Cathy?"

"I don't know!" Cathy exclaimed. She doubted Chris and Lisa would actually have sex, but she assumed Jason had brought it up to see her reaction to the word.

Jason laughed. "What about you, Sartelli? Any luck with Mayor Angeletti's daughter?"

Bryan blushed. "Courtney's not like that," he said.

"You are so in love with that girl," Jason said and shook his head. "The patience you have is unbelievable."

Bryan smiled, and Cathy knew he was done talking about the subject. She held a lot of respect for Bryan because of the way he handled the situation with Courtney. She assumed Courtney must be quite beautiful to have captivated Bryan's unwavering attention.

Jason kicked off his shoes and sat down on the bed with the remote control in his hand. He began scrolling through movie options while Cathy stood awkwardly beside the bed, feeling too nervous to sit down.

"What do you guys want to watch?" Jason asked without peeling his eyes off the TV. "Comedy? Action? Suspense?"

"Honestly, I probably won't be staying long, so you guys should just pick something you like," Cathy reasoned.

Jason turned around to face her. "Sit down already. Get comfortable. You'll be here long enough. Trust me."

You're probably right. Cathy's heart pounded as she stepped out of her high heels and climbed onto the bed beside Bryan. She positioned her back against a decorative pillow and crossed her legs, wishing she had worn pants instead of a dress.

"*Fear and Loathing in Las Vegas*, anyone?" Jason asked.

Bryan laughed. "That may horrify Cathy."

"*The Godfather*?"

"What about something tamer?" Bryan suggested and glanced at Cathy. "What do you like?"

"Pretty much everything, but I love sports movies," Cathy replied.

"See if they have *Friday Night Lights* or *Remember the Titans*," Bryan said to Jason.

"I like the way you think!" Jason cried. "*Friday Night Lights* is actually one of my favorites. I'm sure it's on here," he said while searching for the title. After finding it, he pushed himself further back on the bed and slid to the other side of Cathy. "Hello!" he cried with a child-like grin.

Cathy laughed. She had never been more excited to watch a movie in her life.

CHAPTER 36

AN HOUR-AND-A-HALF LATER, CATHY was sitting on the bed between Bryan and Jason, honestly thinking much more about Jason than the movie playing before her eyes. When it had begun, Jason had positioned himself an inch or two further away from Cathy than his current position. She wondered if he was purposely getting closer to her or if he was doing it subconsciously.

When the credits began to roll, Cathy glanced at the clock on the nearby nightstand: 1:09 A.M. "Wow! Lisa might really make her brother wait until two to pick us up."

Jason smirked. "There's a good chance Lisa may not call her brother at all."

Cathy widened her eyes.

Jason laughed. "I bet when she called her dad, she told him she was going to sleep at your house."

Cathy's stomach dropped.

"No way, dude," Bryan said and shook his head.

Jason smirked. "We'll just have to see."

Butterflies began fluttering in Cathy's stomach. If Lisa intended to spend the night at Chris's, Cathy would have no choice but to stay. She doubted Lisa would deceive her like that, but she couldn't deny that it was a possibility.

"They probably don't even know where we are," Bryan reasoned. "For all we know, they could be downstairs with Jordan."

"They're in bed," Jason stated flatly.

Bryan laughed. "You don't know that, dude."

Jason's eyes glimmered. "Well, let's go find out."

Cathy followed Jason and Bryan out of the guest room and down the long second-floor hallway. The noise from the party below grew louder as they neared Chris's bedroom. Considering how late it was, Cathy was surprised that so many people were still there.

Jason turned to face her and Bryan once they reached Chris's door. He smiled at Cathy before knocking loudly. No response. After ten seconds, he knocked again. "I bet they fell asleep," Jason gathered.

"Dude! Open up!" Bryan called.

"So, knock louder," Cathy stated flatly and banged on the door. "Lisa! Are you in there?"

"Chris was taking shots of whiskey. He's passed out cold by now," Jason reasoned. "I might regret doing this," he muttered as he turned Chris's doorknob. Nothing.

"Locked?" Cathy asked.

"Locked," Jason replied.

"Let's go see if they're downstairs," Bryan suggested. "I doubt Lisa would leave Cathy stranded like that."

"I think Lisa is capable of anything," Jason commented in an amused manner and glanced at Cathy.

She quickly looked away from him. "Let's just check downstairs," she said and stepped past him.

When they reached the first floor, Cathy was stunned that so many high school kids were still present. *Doesn't anyone have a curfew?* She assumed Taylor and his friends were still going strong in the basement, and she wondered if the bash would go all night. If Lisa did intend for them to stay over, where would Cathy sleep?

"Let's check the basement," Jason called over the loud chant of the party.

"Taylor's friends are going to wonder why a bunch of thirteen-year-olds are crashing their party," Bryan commented.

"Who cares?" Jason replied and continued walking toward the basement door.

"At least we're sober. Taylor will be happy about that," Cathy reasoned.

"If he even notices," Jason said as he opened the basement door.

Cathy felt nervous as she entered the basement. The occupants were nearly eight years older than her, and to say she felt out of place was an understatement. To her left were a pool table and a beer pong table; to her right were three couches and a giant flat-screen TV; and against the wall ahead of her was a mahogany bar. To Cathy's surprise, the scene was less rowdy than the one upstairs.

Cathy peered around the area for any sign of Chris or Lisa. She realized that Lisa could have unintentionally fallen asleep, and if that was the case, then her brother was probably growing concerned. Her family would likely call Cathy's parents, and that would be a huge problem... but she couldn't call her parents, right? They would get upset with her for staying at the party later than planned and surely hold it against Lisa. Then they might forbid Cathy from hanging out with her. Lisa was Cathy's closest friend— that couldn't happen! Cathy wracked her brain for a solution. She had not memorized Lisa's phone number, so calling her brother was not even an option.

"Taylor's over there," Bryan said, pointing toward the bar and interrupting Cathy's contemplation. "I don't see Chris."

"Let's ask him what bedrooms are free for the night," Jason suggested. "We might be needing more than one."

Cathy was impressed by how comfortable Jason seemed in the midst of so many older kids. He exuded confidence. She followed him to the back of the room, where Taylor was sitting on a barstool, telling his friends a story. One of the guys nodded towards them as they approached the bar, causing Taylor to look their way. "What's up, guys?" he asked and spun his stool in their direction.

"Chris disappeared with Lisa, and we don't know where to crash," Jason replied.

"He what? Wait, you girls are still here?" Taylor asked, suddenly noticing Cathy's presence.

Cathy felt her cheeks begin to burn. "We're supposed to leave soon," she said quietly.

"Yeah, but we can't find Chris or Lisa. His room is locked, and he's not answering the door," Jason explained.

Taylor rolled his blue eyes. "Do you want me to go bang on his door until he answers?" he offered.

Cathy was about to say "yes" when Jason blurted out, "We just need to know where to sleep in case Cathy has to stay over."

Cathy closed her mouth. *He wants me to stay.*

"Oh. Well, I'm staying in my aunt and uncle's room," Taylor replied. "Jordan took Katie's room. Other than that, you can take any free bed you see."

Jason nodded. "Okay, cool."

"Hopefully it doesn't come to that," Taylor remarked, locking his blue eyes on Cathy. "You girls are way too young to be sleeping over this house."

Cathy blushed.

Jason laughed. "Well, Cathy doesn't want to, but Lisa sure does."

"Try to wake him up again," Taylor said, "and let me know if you need me to step in."

"Will do. Thanks, T," Jason stated and turned toward Cathy and Bryan. "We've got to get upstairs and claim beds before the high school kids start passing out."

"We need to wake up Lisa!" Cathy exclaimed. "What if she didn't tell her dad she was sleeping at my house? What if she accidently fell asleep and her brother is still waiting to hear from her? I will get in *so much* trouble if I end up staying here. My parents will freak out."

"I don't know if I buy that," Jason said and shook his head. "Lisa's pretty smart. She wouldn't leave her brother hanging. Either she's going to come find you before two o'clock or she told her dad she was staying at your house."

"Chris gave her a shot or two of Fireball," Cathy said. "She might not have been thinking clearly."

"Let's try to wake them up, dude," Bryan said to Jason. "As fun as a sleepover would be, we can't let Cathy get in trouble."

"Oh, she's not going to get in trouble," Jason asserted confidently. "We'll figure something out."

CHAPTER 37

CATHY FOLLOWED JASON AND Bryan up to the second story of Chris's home, where they proceeded to bang on his door until they heard movement from inside the room. A few seconds later, Lisa opened the door. "Hi," she whispered.

Cathy widened her eyes. "What the heck, Lis! When are we going home?"

Lisa was wearing a t-shirt much too large for her slim figure and a pair of gray sweatpants. It was clear that she had been sleeping. "I'm sorry. I fell asleep," Lisa replied.

"Well, can you call your brother to come get us?" Cathy asked. "It's almost two."

Lisa bit her bottom lip and glanced from Cathy to Jason and then back to Cathy. "Don't be mad, but I told him not to come."

"What?!" Cathy exclaimed before dropping her jaw.

"He's going to pick us up in the morning," Lisa explained.

"How is your dad okay with that?" Cathy asked.

"My dad's sound asleep. He left Joe in charge," Lisa replied.

"How is your *brother* okay with that?" Cathy questioned her.

Lisa shrugged. "He trusts me—I guess."

Cathy widened her eyes. "My parents are going to ground me forever for this."

"Oh, they're not going to find out," Lisa assured her. "My dad's not going to call them. He's completely aloof."

But I can't keep this from them, Cathy thought. She looked at Lisa with concern and swallowed the large lump in her throat. "I'm not comfortable lying to them, and if I tell them it was your idea, they'll say I can't hang out with you anymore."

"Well, don't do that!" Lisa cried.

"Well, what do you want me to do? Either I have to mislead my parents or get in a lot of trouble. Either option stinks," Cathy retorted.

"Just don't say anything," Lisa suggested. "As long as my brother picks us up in the morning, you'll be back at my house before your mom picks you up for church. She'll assume you slept over. She's not going to be like, 'Oh, did you happen to spend the night at Chris's house?'" Lisa had a point, but Cathy knew she would feel horrible keeping a secret from her parents.

"Lis, you're putting her in an awfully tough spot," Jason said and raised his eyebrows at her.

"Yeah, you are," Bryan agreed.

"Sorry," Lisa said defensively. "I thought you'd be happy to spend the night."

Cathy lowered her eyebrows. "Why would I want to do that?"

Lisa glanced from Cathy to Jason and then shrugged. "I don't know. I just had a feeling."

Cathy knew Lisa was implying that she wanted to spend time with Jason. In all honesty, Cathy did want to spend the night—Lisa could read her well—but not at the expense of lying to her parents. "Can you please call Joe and ask him to come get us?" she pleaded.

"Fine," Lisa acquiesced and pulled Chris's door shut behind her. "I'm not sure he's even awake, but I'll call him."

"I'm coming with you," Cathy said.

"There's a phone in the study," Jason said. "We'll scope out the sleeping options while you guys make your call. Good luck."

When Cathy entered the study a moment later, she shut the door behind herself and Lisa. "I can't believe you lied to me!" she cried angrily.

Lisa let out a short laugh. "I didn't lie to you. I said he would pick us up whenever we wanted."

"You never mentioned that could be in the morning!" Cathy exclaimed.

"I didn't lie to you," Lisa repeated and shook her head. "I just omitted information, which is exactly what you need to do when you see your parents tomorrow."

Cathy sighed. Jason had been right: Lisa was capable of anything.

Knowing that Jason had only hung out with her a handful of times, Cathy was impressed that he could read her so well. Clearly, he was not only book-smart, but also people-smart.

Lisa picked up the phone and dialed her brother's number. "He's not answering," she said after a few seconds.

"Leave a voicemail," Cathy stated sternly.

"Hey, it's me," Lisa said into the phone a moment later. "Call me if you're still up. Chris's number is on the fridge. Everything's fine, so no worries. If you get this in the morning, just pick us up at nine. We'll be ready. Thanks, Joe. Bye." Lisa hung up the receiver and smiled at Cathy. "Are you happy now?"

Cathy crossed her arms. "If he calls back, you won't even know. Anyone in this house could answer the phone, and ninety percent of the people here have no idea who you are."

Lisa sighed. "Let's wait by the phone for five minutes. If he doesn't call, let's assume he's asleep."

"Fine," Cathy agreed and took a seat at the table, which was still set up from their earlier game of Catan. She could not believe how much had transpired since then. Never had she imagined she'd be sitting in the same chair at two o'clock in the morning.

"Don't be mad at me," Lisa said and sat down beside Cathy. "I did this for you, too, you know."

"What?"

Lisa cocked her head to the side. "Jason's into you, and he's hot."

"He's not into me," Cathy stated flatly. "He's a flirt."

"He's into you," Lisa insisted. "Even Chris thinks so."

Cathy's stomach fluttered. "If he is, then he just wants to make out with me. From what I've heard, he's not the type to go out with one girl. I'm not going to hook up with him, so there's really no point in me staying the night."

"You want to. I know it. Don't deny it," Lisa said and smiled mischievously.

Cathy began wondering if Lisa was psychic or just exceptionally good at reading body language. She wasn't sure if Lisa had been insinuating that Cathy wanted to stay the night or that she wanted to make out with Jason, but in complete transparency, both were true. However, she knew better than to hook up with him if she wanted a chance at becoming his girlfriend.

The door to the study swung open a moment later as Jason and Bryan appeared in the doorway.

"Any luck?" Jason asked.

"I left him a voicemail," Lisa replied. "We're just waiting to see if he calls back."

"This late? Unlikely," Jason concluded.

"He could still be awake," Cathy reasoned. "He's in college. Look at Taylor and his friends."

"Yeah, but Joe's only home because he's helping my dad research a case this weekend," Lisa said. "He's doing an internship with my dad's law firm. I bet he fell asleep before midnight."

"Fantastic," Cathy said dryly.

"Well, both guest rooms on this floor are available, so you'll have a room if you need one, Cathy," Jason informed her. "But you should claim it—fast."

"You can sleep on Chris's futon, if you want," Lisa offered.

Cathy shot Lisa a look of disbelief.

"What?!" Lisa laughed. "We wouldn't hook up with you in the room."

Cathy smirked. "I'll take the guest room."

"I don't blame you," Bryan remarked.

"I just want to wait a little longer to see if Joe calls back," Cathy said. "Then I'll go to bed."

"Too bad we couldn't finish our game of Catan," Jason stated. "Do you guys want to sit in for Chantal and Alyssa?" he asked, looking back and forth from Lisa to Bryan.

"I want to go to bed," Lisa responded flatly.

"Sorry, dude, but I'm ready to crash," Bryan said. "I've been up since eight because of baseball."

"Okay, fine. So, Cathy and I will just find something else to do while we wait for Joe to call back," Jason said.

"You just said he was unlikely to call!" Cathy exclaimed.

Jason laughed. "True, but I didn't say it was impossible! Let Lisa go back to bed and Bryan claim a room. We can play a game while we wait and see if he calls." Jason's blue eyes glimmered with excitement, and Cathy tried her hardest to hide the emotions that she was feeling.

"Sounds good to me!" Lisa cried. "I'll leave the door unlocked in case you have to wake me up. Chris is passed out and fully clothed. You won't be walking in on anything."

Cathy sighed. "Fine."

After Lisa and Bryan left the room, Cathy's stomach filled with butterflies. She didn't know what to expect from Jason.

"Want to play Rummy 500?" Jason proposed in a rather childlike manner.

Cathy shrugged. "Whatever," she replied, purposely sounding unenthusiastic.

"You're pissed, huh?" he asked while retrieving a deck of cards from a nearby bookshelf full of games.

"I'll get over it," Cathy replied. "I just have to figure out the best way to tell my parents about what happened."

"You're really that honest, aren't you?"

Cathy shrugged. "I try to be. It's the right thing to do."

Jason smiled. "Chris said you and Chantal were both good girls. He wasn't kidding."

"My parents are usually pretty understanding. When Chantal accidently drank spiked punch, she told them everything. They didn't even ground her."

Jason squinted in thought. "That's a little different. If you tell them about tonight, they're going to wonder why you didn't call them for a ride home."

"I know," Cathy said. "That's why I have to think of a tactful way to explain *everything*. I'm afraid they'll forbid me from hanging out with Lisa, and she's, like, my best friend."

He took a seat in the chair beside her and pushed the Catan board away from them. "So, you just have to decide what's more important: keeping your best friend or telling your parents everything that happens to you?"

As she looked into Jason's eyes, her heart pulsated. She realized what Chantal had been describing for years had finally happened to her: the butterflies, the hot flashes, the heart flutters. Chantal had always been the boy-crazy one—in love with Jon Anderson since age eleven with an ever-drifting eye toward Andy Rosetti. Boys had been capturing Chantal's attention for years. Cathy, on the other hand, had never had anyone pull on her heartstrings. There were boys she found attractive; however, interacting with them had never given her a physical reaction. Everything about Jason— his laugh, his smile, his sparkling blue eyes—made Cathy feel alive in a way she had never experienced.

Escaping her daze, she realized his statement warranted a response. "I'll figure it out," she replied, hoping she did not appear as flustered as she felt.

Jason began shuffling the deck of cards. "Lisa's crafty," he warned. "I'd try my best to stay on her good side."

"She's not vindictive," Cathy remarked, "just eerily intuitive."

"You are too," Jason commented and looked her directly in the eye. "That's what we do. We read people."

"We?"

"People like us," Jason said and put the stack of cards down on the table. He sent a playful look in her direction. "We know what's going on beneath the surface of things."

Cathy lowered her eyebrows. "You don't even know me."

Jason smiled. "Yeah, I do."

Cathy laughed and shook her head. "No, you don't."

"But I do," Jason insisted, "and you know me, too."

"I do?" Cathy questioned him, wondering what type of game he was trying to play with her mind.

Jason nodded.

"I know some things about you, but I don't know enough to pass judgement on you," Cathy stated honestly.

"I'm not talking about judging each other," Jason said. "I'm talking about the feeling I get when I look at you."

At the sound of Jason's words, chills spread throughout Cathy's body. She widened her eyes, trying to quickly think of something to say in return. She wondered if he said such things to every girl he tried to hook up with or if he was actually feeling the same way as her. "What are you, like, some mystic who thinks we knew each other in a past life or something?" she asked sarcastically, trying to gain her composure.

Jason laughed and looked down at the cards on the table. "I bet you've heard horrible things about me," he said in a joking manner, although Cathy could tell he was serious.

"Like what?" she asked, gazing at him with curiosity.

He locked his eyes on her. "Oh, probably something about girls and my penchant for teasing Jon about his religion."

Cathy let out a short laugh. "Sounds like you want to get some things off your chest."

"For the record—and I'm not saying this because I know you go to church—I think church is good for Jon. I tease him because I enjoy hearing him defend himself. He's been inviting me, Chris, and Bryan to youth group for years. Chris has no interest in spiritual things; Bryan's family is pretty involved in their own church; and I already go to church five days a week at school, so the idea of spending the weekend there just doesn't appeal to us."

"Chantal might have mentioned that you like to give Jon a hard time," Cathy said with a smile.

"Knew it," Jason said and snapped his fingers. "And the girls... You've heard about the girls?"

Cathy raised her eyebrows. "What girls?"

"The girls I've hooked up with at Chris's parties," he replied matter-of-factly.

Cathy widened her eyes, a bit in awe of Jason's candor.

"People talk, Cathy. I wasn't around for, like, three months. That gave my friends plenty of time to tell you about me."

Cathy smirked. She wasn't about to bring up anything she had heard about Jason's sex life.

Jason raised his eyebrows at her expectantly. "You're close with Jon. He thinks I'm a man-whore."

"He's never actually said that."

Jason laughed. "Well, he's said it to me."

Cathy raised her eyebrows. "Are you a man-whore?"

"I know I'm a man. Define 'whore,'" Jason immediately responded.

Cathy blushed bright red. "I'm not doing that!" she exclaimed.

Jason laughed. "Then, I don't know what to tell you."

She had expected him to flirt with her in some way once they were alone, but Jason's approach was a bit surprising. He certainly knew how to catch her off guard. She wanted to ask him what feeling he got when he looked at her, but she knew he had said that as bait—whether it was true or not. If she questioned him about it, he would know she had interest in him, and she could not allow that. One of the many pieces of advice that her father had given her over the years had been specifically about boys. He had told her to remember that she was a treasure and to think of herself as a prize that needed to be earned. He said men appreciate what they work hard to attain and often take for granted things that come easily.

"It doesn't look like Joe's going to call back after all," Cathy stated abruptly, purposely changing the subject. "I better claim a bedroom while I still can." She pushed her chair out from the table and stood up.

Jason rose from his seat beside her. "Oh, I guess Rummy can wait. Rummy, Catan, and Manhunt. Wow! We have a lot of future plans!"

Cathy laughed.

"You've had a rough night," he said and hung his arm around her neck. "I'll show you to your room."

"Thanks," Cathy said and allowed him to lead her out of the study.

"Woah. What are *you* still doing here?" Jordan questioned Cathy as she and Jason stepped into the hallway. He was standing, shirtless, in a doorway across the hall. Cathy's eyes widened at the sight of his toned abs.

"No worries. We're heading to separate bedrooms," Jason replied before Cathy could speak.

"Wait. Did Chris get Lisa to stay over?" Jordan asked curiously.

"That, he did," Jason sang.

Jordan laughed. "His A-game is on!"

Cathy heard a female voice and glanced past Jordan into the bedroom. There were two girls sitting on a queen-sized bed, likely hoping to hook up with him.

"He takes right after you," Jason commented.

Jordan laughed. "So, that means you got the shaft, Cathy?"

Cathy was surprised he knew her name. "I was told a half hour ago that we were staying here instead of at Lisa's," she replied.

Jordan's light blue eyes filled with concern. "Are you okay with that?"

Cathy was surprised by the kindness she saw in his eyes and that he even cared to ask. "I guess I have to be," she responded.

"I can give you a ride home if you want," Jordan offered.

Cathy lowered her eyebrows. She was stunned by two things: (1) that he was being so nice and (2) that he would consider driving after drinking all night long.

Jason laughed. "She's probably safer here than getting in your Jeep."

"I'm actually not even drunk," Jordan said. "Seriously, if you need a ride, just knock on this door."

Cathy cocked her head to the side and looked at Jordan strangely, wondering if he was joking. Maybe she was wrong to assume he had been drinking all night? He did look and sound more sober than most of the high school kids she had seen at the party.

"She'll be fine in the spare room," Jason said and put his hand on Cathy's back. "Besides, you have company," he added and nodded toward the bedroom.

Jordan laughed. "All right. Good night, guys."

"Thanks for the offer," Cathy called before following Jason down the hallway.

Once Jordan disappeared into the bedroom and shut the door, Jason stopped walking and turned to Cathy. "MLH's Homecoming King just offered to leave two girls in his bed and drive you home. How special do you feel right now?"

Cathy stopped next to him and smiled. "Why was he being so friendly?"

"Jordan's always friendly," Jason replied, sounding somewhat surprised by her question.

"Really? He's always seemed arrogant to me."

Jason shook his head. "Jordan? No way. He's the nicest Dunkin brother. Chris is closest with Jordan."

"I guess I've never really talked to him," Cathy admitted.

"You've just heard stuff from Jon?" Jason gathered.

Cathy nodded.

"Yeah, Jon's scared of him."

"Why?"

"I have no idea."

"I don't believe you," Cathy stated. "You always have an idea!"

"Oh, so, you know me now?!" Jason teased her.

Cathy giggled.

Without warning, Jason grabbed Cathy's waist with both of his hands and lifted her off the ground. "I'll carry you to your sleeping chambers, Madame," he said in a playful tone. "Hang on."

She knew she shouldn't, but she couldn't help herself; she wrapped her arms around Jason's neck as he positioned her to be carried like a bride. Once she was secure, he began jogging down the hallway and laughing. He ran into a dark bedroom, turned the light switch on with his elbow, and then paused in front of a queen-sized bed. Before Cathy knew what was happening, he tossed her down onto the bed. She landed softly on her back against a few pillows and a down comforter.

"How's that for service?" Jason asked and crossed his arms.

Cathy laughed and kicked off her shoes.

"Well, my work is done for the evening," Jason said. "I'm going to sleep head to toe with Bryan, and maybe I'll see you in the morning."

"Okay. Thank you," she called as he walked out of the room. As much as she enjoyed his company, she was glad that he had left without trying to kiss her. This showed that he (1) respected her and (2) was perhaps interested in more than just a random hookup.

CHAPTER 38

ASON LAY IN BED a few moments later, trying to sort out his thoughts. As well as he could read people, he honestly could not distinguish if Cathy was into him or not. The longer they had interacted, the more his attraction toward her had intensified. She was not only fun, witty, and down-to-earth, but also tactful. She seemed to be unaware of how outwardly beautiful she was, and her humility made her even more alluring.

The feeling that had overcome him when he looked into her eyes was unprecedented. She had somehow made his heartbeat audible. A surge of emotion had shot through his body each time she smiled at him, and he knew there was something unique between them—a connection of some sort. He saw a partner in Cathy, a mind-mate, and, perhaps, even more than that. However, he was torn.

He could tell by Cathy's morals that she would not hook up with him unless they were in a relationship. The idea of committing to any girl was uncomfortable because no female had ever been able to keep his interest for longer than a few weeks. If they were to date and break up, that would make it awkward for their entire group of friends, and Jason did not want to deal with that type of drama. He reasoned that it would be safest to keep his distance from Cathy, but if he chose not to pursue her, then he would never get to explore the visceral connection he sensed between them.

He rolled over on his side and tried to clear his mind so he could fall asleep. *Why am I this torn up over someone I just met six hours ago?* He quickly realized sleep was a lost cause and that he wasn't going to get any rest until he decided how to proceed with Cathy.

CHAPTER 39

CATHY AWOKE SUNDAY MORNING to Lisa nudging her in the side. "Cath, wake up. My brother's going to be here in fifteen minutes."

Cathy creased her eyes open. Lisa looked as vibrant as the sunlight pouring into the guest room. "How are you so awake?"

"Chris woke me up an hour ago."

"Ha. I'm sure he knew exactly what to do."

Lisa laughed.

"You're wearing Chris's clothes home?" Cathy questioned her.

"Yeah. Why not?"

"Won't your brother think you slept in Chris's bed?"

Lisa shrugged. "I don't care what he thinks."

Cathy squinted in thought. She could imagine that growing up without a mother had been difficult for Lisa and that raising a daughter without a wife must have been a formidable task for Mr. Ankerman. Even so, Cathy was continually amazed by the leeway Lisa was given at their age.

"Last night, Jason said he thought you and Chris would end up having sex," Cathy said, hoping Lisa would realize how bad sleeping in Chris's bed made her look.

Lisa let out a short laugh. "That's just because Jay's not a virgin. He thinks everyone who sleeps next to each other ends up having sex. According to Chris, Jay's hooked up with quite a few girls. Chris, on the other hand, is a gentleman."

"Is he?"

Lisa nodded. "I think I'm actually more aggressive than him, and I'm not planning to lose my virginity to my first boyfriend."

"Well, it looks that way," Cathy remarked as she pulled her messy hair into a ponytail.

"Chris will be honest with everyone," Lisa stated assuredly. "No one is going to think we had sex."

"Bryan didn't think it would happen. Then again, Bryan's never even kissed his girlfriend—or whatever Courtney is to him."

"Jason is the only whore around here," Lisa stated playfully.

Cathy's stomach dropped.

"Aside from Jordan and the two girls he slept with last night," Lisa added.

Cathy rolled her eyes and then hopped out of bed. "Girls swoon over that kid."

"I don't blame them. Jordan's the best-looking guy I've ever met," Lisa stated. "Plus, he's super chill."

"I used to think Jordan and Taylor were horrible for throwing parties and exposing Chris to everything," Cathy admitted as she sat down on the floor and began putting on her shoes, "but now that I've spent some time here, I think they have no idea they're being bad influences on him."

"They do the best they can," Lisa remarked. "For a senior in high school and a junior in college, they're given a lot of responsibility. Chris's parents are to blame for the so-called debauchery that takes place in this house."

"I don't understand how they can basically live in Europe while Chris and Katie grow up in the U.S.," Cathy said and stood up to leave the room.

"Right? And I used to think my family was messed up," Lisa said dryly.

"I feel bad for Chris. Good thing he has friends and cousins who care about him."

"And me," Lisa said as she followed Cathy to the door. "I think I actually might love him, a little. I think."

Cathy laughed. "Yeah. Maybe just a little," she said facetiously.

When the girls entered the kitchen a moment later, they were greeted by Jason, who had apparently decided to cook breakfast. Cathy widened her eyes at the large stack of pancakes on a plate beside the stove.

"What's up, guys?" Jason called as he looked over at them.

"Oh my gosh. Those smell so good!" Lisa cried and headed toward him. "Can I have one?"

"Of course," Jason replied. "I made them for everyone. Bryan's still asleep, and Chris went back to bed, but I figured people would be hungry when they wake up."

Cathy smiled. Whore or not, Jason was considerate.

"Thanks," Lisa said and grabbed a plate. "Cathy, do you want some?"

"Sure, if we have time."

"We always have time," Lisa replied and grabbed a second plate for Cathy. She set the food down at the center island and took a seat.

"What are you girls up to for the day?" Jason asked and leaned against the countertop.

"I'm going to take a nice, long nap," Lisa said. "Cathy's going to church."

Jason locked his blue eyes on Cathy as she sat down beside Lisa. "Well what about later?" he asked.

Cathy shrugged. "I'm sure Chantal is going to be upset about last night. I'll do something to cheer her up."

"Oooh...yeah... you're going home to a mess," Jason remarked.

Cathy nodded.

"Well, I was going to say you girls should come here later to watch the Red Sox game, but I doubt Chantal will want to come over," Jason reasoned.

Cathy's heart fluttered.

"I hope she breaks up with Jon," Lisa stated flatly.

Cathy widened her eyes, a bit in awe of Lisa's frankness. After all, Jon was one of Jason's best friends.

"Why, so she can go out with An-dee?" Jason sang.

"Because I think Jon is being a jerk," Lisa replied matter-of-factly.

"What do you think, Cathy?" Jason questioned her.

Cathy sighed. "I don't know... I'm shocked by the entire situation, and I feel really bad for my sister. She loves Jon, and whether she breaks up with him or not, her heart is going to get broken."

Jason's eyes filled with a look of concern. "Hopefully, he'll come to his senses."

"Chris feels bad," Lisa remarked. "He thinks he pressured Jon into drinking."

"Chris is too nice," Jason stated flatly. "He blames himself for everything."

"No one is to blame but Jon," Cathy said. "Actually, I hope Chantal breaks up with him, too."

Jason raised his eyebrows and let out a short laugh. "Wow. I almost want to come to church with you just to see them interact. I bet he feels so guilty. He's probably afraid Chantal will tell your pastor about what he did."

"She wouldn't do that," Cathy said and shook her head.

A knock on the side-door interrupted their conversation. "That's probably Joe," Lisa gathered and stood up from the island. She looked out the window and then opened the door. "Hi. Want to come in for breakfast?"

Joe stepped into the kitchen and glanced at Cathy and Jason before turning back toward his sister. "I can't believe I'm picking you up *here*. I've partied with the Dunkins before. Dad would freak out if he knew what goes on here."

Lisa smiled. "But he won't find out," she said and hugged her brother.

It had not dawned on Cathy that Joe had gone to high school with Taylor. Suddenly it made sense as to why he had been okay with Lisa staying over. Joe probably idolized Taylor, like every other kid from Montgomery.

"Nice clothes," Joe commented and raised his eyebrows at his sister.

"What? Did you expect me to sleep in a dress?" she retorted.

He shook his head and then glanced at the clock. "I have to get back home to help Dad," he said. "Let's go."

"Call here later if you guys want to hang out," Jason said and set his eyes upon Cathy. "I'll be here all day."

Cathy tore her eyes off Jason and turned toward Lisa.

"I'll call Chris after I wake up," Lisa said. "Thanks for breakfast."

"Anytime," he responded and flashed his beautiful smile.

Although Cathy was excited that Jason wanted to hang out with her again, she felt comforting Chantal needed to be her first priority.

CHAPTER 40

THE GIRLS ARRIVED AT the Ankermans' home an hour before Mrs. Kagelli was due to pick up Cathy. Although she had time to take a shower, dry her hair, and dress in the outfit she had packed for church, she felt dirty. She was overwhelmingly nervous about seeing her mother. Typically, she and Chantal told Mrs. Kagelli *everything*. Cathy believed that their honesty kept them all close. She began wondering if Chantal was going to tell their mother about Jon's behavior or if she would cover for him. Cathy's mother would surely tell Mrs. Anderson, and Jon would get in an enormous amount of trouble if Chantal exposed him.

"When are you going to tell me what happened between you and Jay?" Lisa asked curiously as she lay on her bed, still wearing Chris's clothes, while Cathy finished getting ready.

Cathy shot her a perplexed look. "I have nothing to say about him."

Lisa laughed. "Did he try to hook up with you?"

"No!" Cathy exclaimed.

"Hmmm," Lisa said thoughtfully. "Maybe Chris was right."

Cathy sighed. "About what?"

"He said Jay would treat you differently than the other girls because you're a part of our group."

Cathy shrugged, hoping she appeared careless. "He was nice."

Lisa cocked her head to the side. "Well, I could tell by the way he looked at you this morning that he's sweating you."

Cathy tried hard to stop a smile from spreading across her lips. She didn't want Lisa or any of her friends to know that Jason had captured her eye. She planned to tell her mother and Chantal when the timing was right but no one else. "I know better than to get involved with Jason Davids," Cathy retorted. "You said yourself that he's a whore."

"It's not his fault girls fawn all over him."

"Girls at school fawn all over Andy, but he's not a whore."

Lisa dropped her jaw. "I can't believe you just said that!" she exclaimed. "I think you're starting to come around to the idea of him and Chantal."

Cathy shrugged. "I think I'm just really mad at Jon."

"Andy's better for her," Lisa insisted. "She'll realize it, and you'll realize it soon enough."

"Well there's one thing I know for sure: if Jon's at church today, I'm in for an awkward rest of the morning."

***

When Cathy's mother picked her up at Lisa's house, Chantal was already in the front seat. Not knowing what her sister had shared with their mother, Cathy did not want to mention anything about the party. Gazing at Chantal, Cathy could tell she hadn't gotten much sleep, if any.

"How was your night, Cathy?" her mother asked.

Cathy took a deep breath. "It was fun," she replied. "I finally met that kid Jason, and he made my night interesting."

"Oh, Jon's friend from St. Timothy's?" her mother asked.

"Yeah. He's really smart and actually really nice."

Chantal turned to her. "How late did Jon stay after I left?" she asked.

The sadness in her eyes made Cathy cringe. "He left about a half hour after you."

Chantal sighed. "We haven't talked, but I'll see him soon enough."

"What is *that* supposed to mean?" her mother asked, clearly alarmed by Chantal's melancholy tone.

"I think Jon's acting weird, and I'm worried that he's going to break up with me," Chantal replied.

Cathy could tell by the tone of Chantal's voice that she meant what she said. She wasn't angry with him anymore; she wasn't thinking of breaking up with him; she was afraid of losing him.

"How is he acting?" her mother inquired.

Chantal sighed. "Just different."

So, she's going to cover for him, after all.

Thankfully Cathy's mother did not ask any more questions about the previous night. Like Chantal was covering for Jon, Cathy decided to cover for Lisa. The fact that Chantal hadn't been completely transparent made Cathy feel a little less guilty about it. It was strange, though, realizing that they were both withholding information from their mother.

Jon's family typically sat with the Kagellis during church. This Sunday was no different. Chantal took a deep breath before entering the pew where Jon was sitting with his mother and two younger siblings. Cathy watched as he looked at Chantal; his brown eyes were full of shame. Chantal sat down beside him without saying a word. She looked like she was about to cry. Jon tore his eyes off Chantal and glanced at Cathy. She shot daggers at him—not because he had broken his promise to her, but because he had hurt her sister. He immediately looked away and sighed. The worship team began playing on the altar, which thankfully lifted some of the tension in the air.

Cathy's father and younger sister Stephanie joined them in the row a moment later. She could not bring herself to look at her dad. He would be devastated to hear that she had slept over Chris's house, and the guilt she felt for withholding the truth was suffocating her. However, she had finally bonded with a girl her age, and she treasured Lisa's companionship. The thought of not being allowed to hang out with her scared Cathy into silence.

CHAPTER 41

TYPICALLY AFTER CHURCH CONCLUDED, Cathy's parents would spend time mingling with other couples inside the sanctuary, leaving Chantal and Cathy to socialize with the other teens. As the adults filed out of the pew, Cathy sat frozen beside Chantal, who was peering blankly ahead. Jon sat on the other side of Chantal, looking down at his hands. Cathy assumed the three of them looked incredibly strange, sitting together in silence while everyone around them engaged in cheerful chatter.

Cathy had no idea what to say. She wanted to remove herself from the situation, but she had no one to go talk to. A few of the girls she recognized from youth group were standing near the altar, but Cathy was far too shy to approach them. If she found her parents, they would wonder why she wasn't with Jon and Chantal, which could lead to questions Cathy did not want to answer.

The three of them continued to sit in silence until Chantal cleared her throat. When she began speaking, she sounded like she was on the verge of tears. "Jon, I want to understand what you are going through, and I'm trying hard to understand you, but I cannot make any sense of what happened last night."

Jon sighed. "I'm not in a good place," he said flatly, "and I need to figure out why."

"I can tell you why!" Chantal exclaimed. "You're caving to temptation because you don't want to lose your friends. You're prioritizing them over your relationship with God and with me."

"My friends will accept me whether I party with them or not," Jon retorted. "If anything, Chris tried to talk me out of drinking last night. Jason and Bryan weren't even drinking. My friends—*our friends*—are not to blame for what happened. The decisions I made were my own, and I need to figure out what is going on with me."

Chantal turned away from him and looked at Cathy. She appeared to be at a loss for words and looking for Cathy's input. A lump formed in Cathy's throat. Expressing the thoughts that were running through her mind would only stir up Jon's wrath, and Cathy wanted to avoid intensifying the already dramatic situation.

Chantal turned back to Jon. "Then you should take some time to figure out what's causing you to backslide, because it's killing me to see your light fading. You have always had such strong morals and been a good influence on Chris. If he was trying to talk you out of drinking, then your roles have reversed. I can't be in a relationship with someone who isn't honest with me."

"Chantal, I know that!" Jon cried. "That's why I told you everything last night."

"But you hid things from me for an entire month!" Chantal exclaimed.

"I'm sorry! I told you that last night. I realize now that I should have told you everything from the start. The truth haunted me every day. I haven't felt comfortable around you since Chris's party last month."

"If you really felt guilty for drinking, then you wouldn't have done it again," Chantal concluded, "and you certainly would not have smoked weed!"

"Chantal, be quiet," Jon hushed, turning bright red. "My mom cannot hear about this. I will die."

Chantal let out a heavy breath.

"Promise me, you won't tell anyone who doesn't already know," he pleaded. "Both of you, please promise me that."

Chantal sighed while Cathy glared at Jon. "You have no right to ask us to do anything," Cathy retorted.

"I'm not going to tell my parents," Chantal said. "I'll give you time to figure out what's driving you to act this way. If you can get back on track, we will be fine."

Cathy was in awe of the grace Chantal was extending to him. Clearly, love really did cover a multitude of sins. However, the idea of Chantal and Jon staying together turned Cathy's stomach.

"I need some time," Jon responded, "but I'll figure it out."

"You're too nice, Chantal," Cathy stated as she stood up from the pew. She had heard all she could take. "You don't deserve her, Jon," she added. Without waiting for his response, she walked over to her parents, hoping she could talk some sense into Chantal later that afternoon.

CHAPTER 42

HOURS LATER, CATHY WAS sitting in her bedroom with Chantal, trying to comfort her, when her telephone began ringing. Chantal eagerly reached for the cordless phone on Cathy's nightstand, likely hoping it was Jon.

"Hello?" she called into the receiver. Cathy watched as a perplexed expression spread across Chantal's face. "Who is this?" she asked. "Oh!" she exclaimed a few seconds later and then glanced at Cathy with wide eyes. "Yeah, she's right here. Hold on."

"Who is it?" Cathy asked as Chantal passed her the phone.

"It's Jason," Chantal whispered and sent Cathy a puzzled look.

Cathy's heart began to flutter. Because of everything Chantal was going through with Jon, Cathy had not mentioned anything to her about Jason. "Hello?" she called into the receiver.

"Hi!" Jason replied enthusiastically.

"What's up?" Cathy asked while trying to calm her nerves.

"I got your number from Lisa. I told her I was going to invite you back to Chris's tonight."

Cathy laughed. "You already invited me this morning!"

"Yeah, but you didn't say yes, so I figured I would try again."

Cathy smiled. "I'm a little busy right now, but I could ask my mom about coming over later."

"Are you still tied up with Chantal?"

"Yeah."

"Jon came over after he got home from church and said things were pretty awkward between the three of you."

"That's an understatement."

"He's not here anymore, so don't worry. He said he was going to get in touch with Alyssa and try to sort out his issues."

"That's good. Girls are helpful with that sort of thing, and they've been close for years. She'll give him good advice."

"She's in a tough spot, though, because she's best friends with both Jon and Chantal."

"Well, I'm strictly on one side of the argument, so Chantal's in good hands."

Jason laughed. "Do you think you'll get a break and be able to come back over?"

Cathy's heart pounded. "Um, why don't I talk to Chantal and my mom and then call you back?"

"Okay, sounds great," he said cheerfully.

When Cathy hung up the phone, Chantal was staring at her curiously. "What was that about?" she asked.

Cathy could feel her cheeks begin to redden. "He called to invite me to Chris's house for the Red Sox game."

"Why?"

"Um," Cathy stammered, trying to decide what to share with her sister. She didn't want Chantal to know she had stayed over Chris's in fear that she would tell their parents. "After you left last night, Jason and I hung out the whole time. We, um, get along well."

Chantal widened her eyes. "I'm shocked."

Cathy let out a short laugh.

"Wait. But on the phone, you said he invited you this morning. Did he call you at Lisa's, too?"

Cathy could feel the color draining from her face. She forgot she had said that. "Actually, I saw him before you guys picked me up for church," she admitted.

"He went to Lisa's?"

"No. He cooked us breakfast at Chris's house."

Chantal dropped her jaw. "It sounds like he's into you!" she cried.

"Maybe," Cathy said, putting her head down. "That's what Lisa and Chris think, but I can't tell if he's just trying to hook up with me or if he actually likes me."

"Well, be careful," Chantal warned. "He's a heartbreaker."

"I'm aware."

"So, are you going to hang out with him tonight?"

Cathy shrugged. "I guess if you're okay with it."

"I'll find something to do to distract myself. Maybe Alyssa will want to hang out."

"Jason just said that Jon was hanging out with her."

Chantal looked taken aback. "Really?"

"Yeah, but that's probably a good thing. She'll stick up for you."

"Last night, she said he's been really weird toward her lately."

"I'm just glad I'm not her. It would stink to be stuck in the middle of you and Jon. They've been best friends since elementary school, and you're her closest girlfriend."

"I wonder if she'll tell me what they talk about."

Cathy shrugged. "That's a hard call. If she tells you what he says, then you should assume she told him what you said."

"Good point. Well, if she tells him everything, maybe he'll realize how much he has hurt me."

"How was it when you saw Andy last night?"

"Why would you ask that?"

"Lisa said he came in hopes of talking to you."

"Did he? So, he really isn't over me?"

"Not at all. Lisa said he's been straightedge since he lost you."

"Good!"

"I think if Jon lost you, it would wake him up, too."

Chantal sighed. "I'm hoping he will snap out of it without me breaking up with him. I'm in love with someone who seemingly vanished off the face of the Earth this month. As nice as it is to hear Andy still likes me, my heart belongs to Jon now."

That's unfortunate. "I just want you treated right," Cathy said. "Jon's not acting like the kid you started dating. You two used to pray together, not fight over alcohol and marijuana. From the outside, it is clear you are walking different paths."

Chantal hung her head. "I know."

"I haven't given up on him," Cathy stated. "I think he'll come to his senses, eventually. I just don't want to see you get hurt in the process."

"I can't break up with him. If I do, he will just indulge further into Chris's lifestyle and have no one to hold him accountable."

"Or he'll miss you and realize the error of his ways like Andy did. It could go either way. I guess you should just pray about what to do. Ask God to shut the door on you and Jon if it's not His will," Cathy reasoned. "Be open to whatever happens."

Chantal sighed. "I just dread the door shutting."

"If it does, it's for a reason. Listen to the still, small voice inside your heart. You know how to do that."

"What is 'the still, small voice' saying about *Jason Davids*?" Chantal asked in an amused manner as her countenance brightened.

Cathy blushed. "I haven't had a chance to pray about him yet. I guess I'm still trying to process what happened last night. He said he feels like we already know each other and that he gets some sort of feeling whenever he looks at me. I didn't ask him to elaborate, even though I wanted to know what he meant. I felt something, too. It was strange."

"What did you feel?"

Cathy looked away from her sister; she hated verbalizing her emotions. "I guess I felt intrigued... and... happy," she described.

"So, you like him back?"

"I guess."

"Go over Chris's house," Chantal urged her and widened her eyes excitedly. "You have good discernment. You'll be able to tell if Jay's playing you or not."

"Okay. I'll go talk to Mom about it. Are you sure you'll be okay?"

Chantal nodded. "I'll spend some time in prayer and find some peace."

Cathy appreciated Chantal's selflessness and believed alone time would be good for her twin. Now she was tasked with having to ask her mother to drive her to Chris's house, which would entail telling her about Jason. It had always been difficult for Cathy to verbally express her emotions, especially ones deeply felt.

CHAPTER 43

***

FOR THE NEXT FEW weeks, Jason continued to pursue Cathy. They were able to fulfill all their plans: Manhunt, Catan, Rummy, and other games that captured their analytical minds. Cathy quickly realized she had found a mind-mate in Jason—someone intuitive like herself, who got bored easily and loved to be challenged. Jason's outgoing and confident personality brought balance to Cathy's life. She no longer had to ease into unfamiliar situations because Jason led her through them.

It did not take long for news to travel around youth group that Cathy had been spending a lot of time with Jason. Montgomery was small, and Jason's family was well known because of their affluence. His less than spectacular reputation was also known and, perhaps, best perpetuated by the plethora of girls who had crushes on him.

Rumors began to spread, and it was not long before most of the youth group believed Cathy was hooking up with Jason. Because physical relationships at such a young age were frowned upon, Cathy was accused of backsliding—yet she had never even kissed him. She despised being the center of attention, and the gossip was making her dread attending church. Although Chantal came to Cathy's defense, Chantal had issues of her own to address.

Word had spread around Montgomery Lake Middle School about Chris's parties. A decent amount of the youth group kids attended there, which meant they had heard multiple rumors about Jon drinking and fighting with Chantal. Jon felt humiliated, and Chantal felt drained from constantly coming to his defense. The fact that Jon was feeling less and less comfortable at church was only making him gravitate more and more toward Chris's house. Chantal could not even hold that against him because she knew he was being treated unfairly at church. He had tried to repent and get back on track, but people would not stop badmouthing him. The idea of grace seemed to evade the minds of the youth group kids, and instead, they judged.

It was not long before both Cathy and Chantal were begging their parents to let them quit youth group. Mrs. Kagelli was a laid-back, non-judgmental person, which made it easy for the girls to confide in her. They ended up sharing *a lot* of details with their mother—nothing about Cathy sleeping over Chris's house or Jon smoking pot—but pretty much everything else that had happened between Cathy and Jason and Chantal and Jon.

"I don't blame you for not wanting to spend time around people who are making up rumors about you. It is not what Christianity is supposed to be about; it is actually the *opposite* of what church should be like," their mother expressed. "It is still important for you to study God's word, so I don't want you dropping out of youth group completely, but I am fine with you just going every other week."

"What's happening doesn't make any sense!" Cathy protested. "Everyone has become obsessed with our lives. They are gossiping, judging, and lying. They are the ones in sin, yet they think we are awful sinners."

"It's really not right," Chantal concluded. "I can't even focus on learning about God because I have to constantly defend my boyfriend and my sister."

"Somehow liking Jason makes me a whore, and Jon slipping up at a party makes him a drunk!" Cathy cried. "Even if the rumors were true, shouldn't we be able to come to church peacefully to seek God's forgiveness?"

"Girls, your points are valid," Mrs. Kagelli said. "I just need to talk this over with your father. Maybe we can find another youth group for you to attend."

"Why can't we just study the Bible as a family?" Cathy suggested. "I already have friends. I don't need to meet new kids from another church. Jason, Lisa, Chris, Alyssa, and Bryan are much nicer than the Christian kids I know."

Mrs. Kagelli sighed. "What if I talk to Pastor Mark about what has been going on? He could step in and set the kids straight. What they are doing is wrong, and they need to be held accountable."

"Maybe if we tell Pastor Mark why we don't want to attend youth group, he'll do a message on gossip and slander," Chantal reasoned.

"I doubt that would help. Clearly, his messages on grace and honesty fell on deaf ears," Cathy retorted.

"Let me talk to your father," Mrs. Kagelli said. "We will figure something out. I don't want your perception of God to become tainted by the imperfections of man."

Cathy rolled her eyes. "Mom, I know God's not the one making up the rumors. I'm not going to blame Him for their cruel lies. This has nothing to do with us wanting space from God. We just want to surround ourselves with people who respect us."

"I can't blame you for that," Mrs. Kagelli commented. "Just forget about this for tonight if you can. Leave it up to me and Dad to find a solution."

After their conversation, Cathy prayed that her parents would not make her continue attending youth group. In addition to what the kids were saying about her, it angered her to hear what they were saying about Jason. In the three weeks they had known each other, he had done nothing to disrespect her. He had not even tried to kiss her. Just because people knew about his history with girls, they assumed he was incapable of treating Cathy with respect.

Up until that day, Cathy had not mentioned the turmoil at church to Jason. She had been afraid it would scare him away because he detested drama. However, when he came over that evening to play Risk with her, Chantal, and Jon, he read her like an open book.

"What's going on?" he asked while they waited in the dining room for Chantal and Jon. "Something's bothering you."

"I don't want to bring you into it," Cathy replied and looked away from him. "It's just drama at church."

"Because of Jon and Chantal?"

"Partially."

"Because of me?"

Cathy locked her eyes on him. "Why would you think that?"

"Because people love to talk about me, and it's not a secret that we've been hanging out."

Cathy bit her bottom lip and eyed him apprehensively.

"My brother explained this to me last year," Jason began. "He said if you're popular people will consume themselves with your business and make you feel picked apart. I know you haven't met him yet, but girls *love* my brother Luke. Some people in his grade resent him for it, so he hangs out with my brother Matt's grade instead."

"What does that have to do with anything?"

"You're going to be the center of attention, Cathy. You're beautiful, funny, and smart. For the rest of your life, there will be people who judge you and hate you for no reason at all. They will look for reasons not to like you. When they can't find any, they will make them up."

"That's a terrible fortune!" she exclaimed and widened her eyes.

"I'm just trying to say that jealousy makes people cruel, and people are jealous of you."

"No. People think I'm hooking up with you and that I'm a terrible Christian."

Jason shook his head. "They don't really believe that. They just want to think that. The sooner you learn to block out other people's opinions of you, the happier you'll be."

"I don't want to go church anymore," Cathy admitted. "I can't stand the way people are treating me, Jon, and Chantal. It's giving me anxiety."

"You don't need organized religion to feel at peace with yourself. I know your faith is important to you, but God is everywhere—well, except for maybe at your church, considering the way people treat each other," Jason said sarcastically.

Cathy laughed. "My mom might let us quit youth group. Chantal and I talked to her about it earlier. She's going to figure things out with my dad. Honestly, even before this, I never felt welcome there."

"It goes back to what I told you. People are jealous of you. It's no secret that you're a straight-A student and an awesome athlete."

"Thanks."

"And now, I'm sure girls are jealous that you hang out with me, Chris, Bryan, and Jon. The fun is wherever the Dunkins are, and everyone knows that in Montgomery."

"You guys are so much nicer than the kids at my church."

"That's because we're self-centered."

Cathy laughed.

Jason smirked. "No, but seriously, we're too busy living our lives to waste time talking about other people. None of us focus on people beyond our group of friends. It makes us pretty self-absorbed but evidently nicer than everyone else."

Cathy smiled. "You have so much perspective. Thanks for talking this through with me. I feel a little better."

"Good! Now, what do you think the odds are that Chantal and Jon got in an argument and that's why they're nowhere to be found?"

"Pretty high. Chantal's a little weirded out that he's been spending so much time with Alyssa."

"I think he's just trying to go back to his roots and figure himself out. Alyssa is like a sister to him."

"I've seen the way he hugs her and the way he looks at her. I don't think Chantal's crazy to be concerned."

Jason shook his head. "Jon loves your sister—no one else. Alyssa's a comfort to him, and he's thankful for her, but his heart belongs to Chantal."

"If that's true, he has a strange way of showing it."

"He's a strange kid in general," Jason remarked.

"True," Cathy said slowly. "Let's go look for them. If they're not up for playing Risk, we can just watch a movie or something."

As she stood up to leave the room, Jason tugged on her arm. "Wait," he said.

"What?" she asked and sat back down.

"Why do you still hang out with me?"

"Huh?"

"You're being badmouthed for spending time with me. Why is it worth it to you?"

Cathy widened her eyes. She had no idea how to respond. The idea of not hanging out with him to stop the rumors had never even occurred to her.

"I guess what I'm trying to figure out is why you're letting yourself go through this just to be my friend," he added.

A pit formed in her stomach. She hated that he had referred to her as a "friend."

"You look like a deer in headlights right now," Jason said and smiled. His blue eyes were filled with wonder.

"I'm sure I do," Cathy responded after swallowing the large lump in her throat.

"I guess what I'm trying to say is it would be more worth it if we were more than friends."

Cathy's heart began pounding in her chest, and she could feel her cheeks turning red. Was he asking her out? Her tongue was tied, and she hoped he would continue talking before expecting a response from her.

"You look a little stunned, and I'm kind of surprised," Jason admitted. "You must know why I've wanted to hang out with you every weekend since we met. This really can't be a surprise to you."

"Um, I'm just not really good with stuff like this," Cathy replied and looked away from him.

"Tell me you feel what I feel. Tell me the connection we share is not just part of my imagination," Jason urged her.

Cathy looked up at him. "I can't tell you if I feel what you feel unless you tell me how you feel."

"Like you're my partner," Jason replied immediately. "I've wanted to kiss you since the night I met you. I am more attracted to you than any girl I know." He looked directly into her eyes as he spoke. "I just didn't want to rush anything because I thought I might scare you away."

Cathy smiled. "You know how to deal with me."

"I didn't want you to think I was just trying to hook up with you," he added and squeezed her hand.

Cathy could feel her cheeks growing warmer and warmer with each word Jason spoke.

"Your morals are different from your best friend's, so I knew I couldn't approach you the way Chris pursued Lisa. I figured getting to know each other as friends was the best way to explore the connection I sensed. I just need to know if you feel it, too."

Cathy took a deep breath. "I do," she admitted in a flat tone.

"You are a pro at concealing your emotions," Jason stated with a smirk. "If I didn't feel such a strong vibe between us, I would have had no idea that you were open to being more than friends."

"Well, I hope your interest in me doesn't wane now that you know," Cathy said facetiously.

Jason's eyes sparkled. "Before I met you, I couldn't imagine myself wanting a girlfriend in middle school. Now, I can't imagine ever losing interest in you."

Cathy couldn't stop a wide smile from spreading across her face.

"Is it okay if I call you my girlfriend?" he asked and again squeezed her hand.

"That would sure make the rumors more worth it!" she laughed playfully.

Jason smiled widely. The way his blue eyes glimmered filled Cathy with excitement. By concealing her feelings until he had expressed his own and by allowing him to do all the pursuing, she had accomplished her goal. Her father had been right: boys cherish what they work hard to attain.

CHAPTER 44

THE FOLLOWING DAY, CATHY's parents informed her and Chantal that they no longer had to attend youth group on Fridays. They felt the girls would benefit more from going to Bible study with them on Wednesdays, which was open to any age but usually only attended by adults. The relief Cathy felt was immense.

"Hopefully Jon's mom won't make him go to youth group if we don't," Chantal said to Cathy after they finished discussing the issue with their parents.

"I doubt Jon told her anything about what's going on. She would worry that the rumors were true," Cathy reasoned. "He should ask her if he can go to Bible study with us instead. If he still seems interested in the Bible, his mom won't be suspicious of anything."

"That's a good idea," Chantal agreed.

"What happened last night? You guys took forever to come downstairs and play Risk."

Chantal rolled her eyes. "We ended up talking about his friendship with Alyssa. I told him that I find it weird he's spending more time with her than me. He—no surprise—got angry."

"Jason said Jon loves only you and that Alyssa is like a sister to him," Cathy said, hoping to put her sister to ease.

Chantal smiled slightly. "I'd like to think that, but what do you think? What does Lisa think?"

Cathy let out a heavy breath. "I haven't talked to Lisa about it, but I can. I think you have a reason to be concerned. I don't think Alyssa would backstab you, but Jon is a loose cannon these days. I think he's capable of anything."

"I trust Alyssa; I just don't trust Jon," Chantal stated.

"In what way?"

"Um, I guess I don't trust him to be honest with me about his feelings. If they keep hanging out every day after school, he could develop more feelings for her than me."

"So, you're questioning how much he really loves you?"

Chantal nodded. "I guess I am."

Cathy looked down in thought. "I'll bounce this off Lisa. She's good at figuring out what's going on beneath the surface of things."

"Tell me what she says."

"You guys seemed fine when we played Risk, so you must have come to some understanding."

Chantal let out a short laugh. "Yeah, an understanding that we had plans with you! We resolved nothing."

"I'm sorry. All you two do is fight lately. It's horrible to watch."

"I'm just afraid if he loses me, he'll backslide."

"You have to put yourself first, occasionally. Saving him from a downward spiral is not worth your peace of mind," Cathy said, hoping her sister would see that her relationship with Jon had become toxic.

"I think his father is the root of the problem," Chantal speculated. "He lives across the country and has nothing to do with his children. Jon has no one to show him how to treat a woman—no example to follow. Plus, he feels abandoned, and I know that's why he clings to his friends so tightly."

"You're probably right," Cathy said, "but he shouldn't take it out on you. You're letting him use you as a punching bag. Remember what Dad told us? 'Guys appreciate things they have to work hard to get.' Jon worked hard to get you in the beginning, but now that he has you, you're making it too easy for him. Your love should be earned."

Chantal rolled her eyes. "I hate mind games."

"Oh my gosh. Are you serious? This has nothing to do with mind games. It's basic human nature. Jon is going to walk all over you until you stand up for yourself!"

"What am I supposed to say to him that I haven't already said?" Chantal asked defensively.

"Um, how about, 'Jon I can't deal with your *craziness* anymore? I'm at my limit.' Or, 'Why don't you just date Alyssa? You spend all your time with her anyway.'"

Chantal dropped her jaw. "I can't say those things to him. He'll think I want to break up!"

"Ugh, Chantal! Why don't you get it? You are a smart girl!" Cathy exclaimed. "Jon thinks you won't break up with him. He thinks he can do *anything* he wants because you've stayed with him for this long. He isn't treating you with the respect you deserve. He shouldn't hang out with his female best friend five days a week and only see you on the weekends."

Chantal's eyes filled with tears. "So, you think he likes her?"

"I think he's valuing her over you," Cathy replied. "That's not the same thing, but it's not good either."

Chantal sighed. "I need to take a nap. I'm emotionally shot."

As Cathy watched Chantal leave the room, she prayed that her sister would find peace. It was bewildering that Chantal had taken such a strong stance against alcohol by leaving Chris's first party but was now struggling to stand up for herself. As Cathy thought more about it, she reasoned that Chantal must have grown insecure about her and Jon's relationship, causing her shift in behavior. When she felt loved by him, she had no problem voicing her beliefs. Now that she was questioning his interest in her, she was afraid to express herself.

A moment later, Cathy went upstairs to her own bedroom, deciding she needed to call Lisa and discuss the situation.

"You finally see it!" Lisa cried after Cathy explained the dilemma. "I've been saying this for months. Jon is not good for your sister!"

"Okay. You were right, but what do you think about Alyssa?"

Lisa let out a heavy breath. "She's a good friend, and she wouldn't backstab Chantal by hooking up with him. He's the one who keeps asking her to hang out, and she feels obligated to help him because she wants things to get better between him and Chantal. She doesn't realize she's a point of contention between them. Chantal needs to talk to her."

"Chantal is shutting down," Cathy said. "She's too intimidated to talk to either one of them."

"That's because he's tearing her apart. The problem isn't that Alyssa is spending so much time with him; the problem is that Jon would rather hang out with Alyssa than Chantal. It doesn't matter if they hook up or not. At this moment, he's more interested in spending time with his best friend than his girlfriend. That is clear."

"What do I do? How do I help her?" Cathy asked, feeling frustrated.

"Try to talk to him. Point out the truth. You're good at that."

Cathy cringed. She hated the idea of conversing with Jon. "So, basically you're saying that my instinct is right? Jon spending this much time with Alyssa is a bad sign?"

"Yes! It's a horrible sign!" Lisa exclaimed. "Chantal should start hanging out with Andy and see how quickly Jon rushes back to her. He's taking her for granted."

"You know what? I am open to that because I like Andy a lot better than Jon right now."

"You should call Jon while you're this fired up," Lisa suggested.

"I'm sure he's at Alyssa's."

"Then leave him a message. He'll call you back. Tell him his behavior is unacceptable. Tell him it appears as though he wants to date Alyssa."

"Okay. Let me go. I'll call him," Cathy said and hung up the phone. She was somewhat afraid Chantal would get mad at her for getting involved, but she felt obligated to stand up for her. Unsurprisingly, she got Jon's voicemail. "Hi, Jon. It's Cathy. I need to talk to you about something. Call me back when you can. Bye," she said in a completely flat tone.

CHAPTER 45

THE FOLLOWING DAY, CHANTAL made plans to go shopping with Alyssa in an attempt to sort things out about Jon. Cathy hoped her twin would convey how bothered she was by Jon's behavior and gain some insight into his and Alyssa's friendship. Meanwhile, Cathy planned to spend the day at Jason's house; he wanted her to meet his family. Although she had heard that Jason's family was affluent, she was stunned when she saw the size of his home.

"Hi!" he greeted her warmly at the front door. "Come in!"

Cathy widened her eyes as she stepped inside his foyer. Two staircases rose up to the second-floor, one on either side of the room, like the inside of a palace. Jason's house made her own four-bedroom home look like a shack. "Your house is so nice," she said while he led her toward the kitchen.

"My mom designed it," Jason stated proudly.

"That's pretty awesome."

"You can tell her because you're about to meet her."

The idea of meeting Jason's parents and brothers for the first time was a bit nerve-wracking, but their warm personalities quickly put Cathy at ease. Jason's mother gave Cathy a hug when Jason first introduced them. His father was also friendly—Jason had his smile. Luke was hot—perhaps just as hot as Jason. He seemed amused by the fact that his little brother had a girlfriend, but nevertheless, he greeted Cathy with a warm embrace. Matt seemed more reserved than the rest of the family but very polite. Jason had told Cathy that he looked up to Matt, who was a leader by nature.

Later while sitting with the Davids in their living room, Cathy couldn't help but wonder if they would still mean something to her a year later. The fact that Jason had wanted her to meet them assured her that he was serious about their relationship—as serious as a thirteen-year-old could be anyway.

When Cathy returned home that night, she had a message from Jon. Her stomach sank. She had just had such a great day with Jason and his family; she really did not want to ruin it by fighting with Jon. Everything she planned to say would upset him, so she knew an argument was on the horizon. Before dialing his number, she considered her choice of words. She needed him to realize Chantal was capable of breaking up with him. *Should I mention something about Andy?* Cathy realized she had so much to say that getting her thoughts in order was not a viable option.

Her hand shook as she dialed Jon's number. Waiting for him to answer, she attempted to calm her nerves. When his voicemail picked up, she let out a sigh of relief. As she was about to end the call, she realized it would be foolish to keep playing phone tag. What she wanted to say really didn't warrant a response, so leaving a message would suffice:

"Hi Jon. I got your message. I want to keep this short and to the point, so I'm just going to say it now. I'm really upset by the way you've been acting lately, and from the looks of things, it seems like you should just be dating Alyssa. It's clear to everyone that you have feelings for each other... I don't think there's anything more to say... Please don't even bother calling me back." With that, Cathy hung up the phone. She hoped her message would help Jon realize a few things: (1) that people thought his friendship with Alyssa was inappropriate, (2) that if she was at her wits end, Chantal could be next, and (3) that he had just lost a friend.

***

A couple of hours later, Chantal rushed frantically into Cathy's bedroom. Tears were streaming from her green eyes, and she looked panicked.

Cathy gasped. "What's wrong?"

Chantal began breathing heavily. "Jon just broke up with me," she sobbed and fell onto Cathy's bed.

"What?!"

"It's even worse. He told me he was going to go out with Alyssa," she heaved.

Cathy dropped her jaw and widened her eyes. "Were you not *just* with Alyssa?"

Chantal nodded.

Cathy dropped her jaw again. "I'm stunned. I left him a message earlier telling him how disappointed I was in him and saying that it looked like he and Alyssa had feelings for each other. I hope that didn't push him over the edge. I was just trying to get him to see how *bad* it is that he's spending more time with her than you."

"I doubt he even cared," Chantal stated and shook her head. "I don't know what hurts more…Jon falling for Alyssa, or Alyssa backstabbing me."

"You need to talk to her," Cathy said. "I'm surprised she would do that to you."

"Why? They've spent the last three weeks together. It really shouldn't be that big of a surprise. I'm just the naïve idiot who didn't want to see it coming!"

"Tal, I'm so sorry," Cathy said and hugged her sister. "He just made a huge mistake, and he's going to regret it for a long time. You are the nicest person I know. He's lost his mind."

After Chantal left Cathy's bedroom to go find their mother, Cathy called Lisa and told her what happened.

"Alyssa would never do that!" Lisa exclaimed. "Chantal has to talk to her. Jon has such a bad temper. He probably just said that out of spite. Did you talk to him yesterday?"

"No. We played phone tag, and then I finally just left him a message saying everything I wanted to say. Now I'm afraid he broke up with her because of what I said."

"He probably broke up with her because he thought you found out he liked Alyssa," Lisa reasoned. "If he wasn't guilty, he wouldn't have broken up with her. Jon may have fallen for Alyssa, but I can't see them dating. I can't see Alyssa backstabbing Chantal. Plus, I always thought she had a thing for Bryan."

"Well, Bryan's clearly in love with Courtney Angeletti, so maybe Alyssa moved on. I'm going to call Jason. Maybe he'll know what's up."

"Keep me posted. I'm going to tell Andy the news."

"Good idea. Maybe he can cheer up Chantal. She's devastated." After Cathy hung up with Lisa, she called Jason.

"That doesn't make any sense," he said after she explained what had happened. "I know he's been acting strange lately, but this is beyond anything I imagined he would do."

"Me, too. I called him to talk about everything yesterday, but he must have been hanging out with Alyssa. He called me back today when I was at your house. When I called him back, I got his voicemail. I kind of let him have it."

"Well, he obviously deserved it. What did you say?"

"I just said that I was upset with the way he's been acting and that it seems like he should be dating Alyssa. I also said it appears they have feelings for each other. I told him not to bother calling me back. I wanted him to know I was through with him, thinking maybe he would start treating my sister better. I didn't expect him to break up with her!"

"I wonder if he thought she asked you to say that. Maybe he got mad, thinking she put you up to it?"

"Maybe, but that's a pretty extreme way to react."

"I'm not even going to call him. I honestly don't want to deal with him anymore. I have an aversion to drama, and Jon stirs it up everywhere he goes," Jason said. "He's exhausting."

"I feel so bad for Chantal. Her best friend might have stolen her boyfriend."

"I don't buy that. I bet Jon just said that to be a jerk. Chantal should verify things with Alyssa before she believes anything he said," Jason reasoned.

"I agree, but I think she's too hurt to think clearly or talk to either one of them."

"So, I guess we won't all be hanging out together anymore," Jason said. "I'm glad I met you before this happened."

Cathy sighed. "Me, too. It's going to be so awkward when Jon's around. I think I hate him."

"I doubt he'll want to show his face around you," Jason stated. "That's fine though. We could use a break from his drama."

"Any advice on how to cheer up Chantal?"

"I've never had my heart broken. I have no idea what helps," Jason replied.

"Me either. I guess I'll just pray for her. Maybe Lisa can set her back up with Andy. I can't believe I'm saying that. I used to hate Andy, but what he did to her wasn't nearly as bad as what Jon has done."

"I don't know a thing about her history with Andy, but if you think that will cheer her up, then go for it."

"Lisa's wanted Jon and Chantal to break up for months. She kept telling me that he wasn't good for her and that Andy was better. I thought she was just trying to help her best friend, but now I realize she just saw everything coming. She's, like, psychic or something."

"She's an INTJ."

"A what?"

"A Myers-Briggs INTJ personality. I learned about it in my psychology class. I find personality types interesting because I'm naturally inclined to read people."

"Well, what am I?"

"You are the rarest of all types. You and Lisa are a lot alike, but you have one crucial difference: you feel other people's emotions; she doesn't."

"Lisa cares about people."

"Oh, I know she does. I'm not saying she's heartless. I'm saying you actually *feel* other people's emotions. You empathize. When someone is upset, it upsets you."

"Well, that's true, so what does that make me?"

"An INFJ."

"I'll have to read up on that. How many personality types are there?"

"Sixteen. The system is based on the cognitive functions people use most often. You and I use the same four functions but in a different order."

"Sounds like you know a lot about this. No wonder you can read people so well," Cathy commented. "What type are you?"

"An ENFJ: the extraverted version of you."

"Oh my gosh. That makes sense!"

Jason laughed. "It really is fascinating when you start learning about it. Anyone with an NF or NT in their personality code usually finds the subject interesting."

"So, Lisa's a T instead of an F—does that mean she's more logical than caring?"

"It means she's in tune with her own values more than those of others, and she makes her decisions without factoring in other people's feelings— like when she made you sleep over Chris's house. It's also why she comes off so cold when you first meet her, and why she doesn't care what people think of her."

"My God. You can read people like open books."

Jason laughed. "Go online and read up on it. I think you'll find it fascinating."

"So, do you think our connection comes from having similar personality types?" she wondered, feeling intrigued by the subject.

"I think that's part of it, but it's definitely more than that. The first night we met, a feeling came over me whenever I looked at you. I can't even articulate it, but it was like a gut feeling that we were meant to be something.

I couldn't shake it."

Cathy smiled. *So that's what you meant.*

CHAPTER 46

To say the next month was rough for Cathy's group of friends was an understatement. Chantal, naturally, pulled away from everyone except for Cathy and Jason. She decided to devote herself to her faith and return to youth group. Without Jon or Cathy there, it was a much more comfortable place. In fact, the kids were nice to Chantal; it appeared they all felt bad for her.

Cathy wanted to avoid Jon and Alyssa at all costs, so she spent most of her time with Jason and Lisa, only going to Chris's house if Jon and Alyssa were not invited. Jason was also trying to avoid the drama by putting space between himself and Jon. Chris was unfortunately caught in the middle. As Jon *and* Jason's best friend, he had to make a lot of choices regarding how he spent his time. Bryan distanced himself from the entire situation and focused on his relationship with Courtney.

Lisa still did not believe Alyssa had hooked up with Jon, but it didn't look good that Jon was continuing to spend all of his time with her after the breakup. However, according to Chris, Jon and Alyssa were not hooking up or dating. Alyssa told Lisa she had no idea who started that rumor, but it was false. She was devastated that Chantal would not speak to her.

Lisa tried to get Cathy to hang out with Alyssa, but Cathy had reservations. Even if Alyssa hadn't backstabbed Chantal, she was still "the other girl." Spending time with her would hurt Chantal—it just couldn't happen.

In the meantime, Lisa worked her magic and got Andy to begin pursuing Chantal again. This was a saving grace because Andy seemed to be the only one capable of lifting Chantal's spirits. Spending time with Andy and his friends gave Chantal a social outlet inside and outside of school.

After Andy began attending youth group and church with Chantal, it became clear a relationship was developing between them. Chantal finally seemed like her vibrant, cheerful self again. Cathy was thankful for Andy, which was rather ironic considering how much she used to detest him. The whole situation with Andy made her realize that she needed to be more gracious, that good people can make mistakes, and that people can change.

CHAPTER 47

ONE JUNE AFTERNOON, JASON called Cathy to share some surprising news: Jon was telling people that Chantal broke up with him.

"What?!" Cathy gasped. "That is insane!"

"I know."

"Is he saying that to come to his and Alyssa's defense? Like, spreading that around their school so people won't talk bad about them?"

"All I know is that he told Chris he thinks it's awful that you and Chantal cut Alyssa out of your lives."

Cathy let out a short laugh. "Are you kidding me? He told Chantal he was going to date her!"

"Cathy, this is bizarre. I think Jon might have actually lost his mind."

"What does Chris think?"

Jason sighed. "Chris is trying to stay out of it, but he thinks Jon and Chantal should talk and clarify things because their stories don't match up. Jon claims that he and Alyssa are just friends."

"What do you think? Aside from the possibility that Jon has lost his mind."

"There is definitely a miscommunication somewhere, but nothing is going to get resolved unless Chantal is open to talking to Jon or Alyssa."

"She's finally happy again," Cathy said. "Talking to them would just open up old wounds. She likes Andy, and he's good to her. They'll be boyfriend and girlfriend in no time. Lisa was right all along: Andy is better for her."

"I've only met him a few times, but I think he's a nice kid and definitely better for her than Jon. I think Alyssa got thrown under the bus in Jon's fit of rage. I don't believe she hooked up with him or had any intention of dating him."

"If that's true, then she lost two of her closest friends for no reason."

"Right."

"I should talk to her," Cathy reasoned, realizing that if Jason and Lisa had the same theory, it was probably true.

"I've been trying to stay out of this, but I honestly feel bad for Alyssa. I've known her for years, and she's not a malicious person."

"I'll talk to Lisa about it. Maybe the three of us girls can get together and figure some things out."

"Cool. Keep me posted. I'm intrigued."

Cathy hung up the phone and paused before calling Lisa. Something was not adding up right. Lisa was the best at figuring out complex situations, so Cathy figured she would shed some light on the topic.

"Hello?" Lisa answered a few seconds later.

"Hey. So, Jason just told me the strangest thing: Jon is telling people Chantal broke up with him."

"What?!"

"Yeah. That was my reaction, too."

"He's such an ass! Is he saying that so people won't judge him for breaking Chantal's heart?"

"I have no idea, but Jason thinks Alyssa had nothing to do with the breakup and that Jon threw her under the bus."

"That's why I've been trying to get you to talk to her. I think Jon made that up because he was pissed," Lisa theorized. "But why was he so pissed? That's what I don't understand. What set him off?"

"My message, maybe?" Cathy suggested. "I expected him to get mad at me, but I never imagined he'd take it out on her."

"I'll reach out to Alyssa and try to make some sense of this," Lisa said. "All I know is that Chantal is way better off now, far away from Jon. Andy's so happy to have her back in his life. He'll treat her right."

"I want to shield Chantal from all of this and anything that has to do with Jon."

"I do, too. I'll call Alyssa and call you back. I won't talk to her if Jon's there. Bye," she said abruptly.

An hour later, Cathy was looking at pictures on Jason's Facebook page, admiring his good looks, when Lisa called her back.

"Holy crap! I think I figured it out," Lisa stated as soon as Cathy answered the phone.

"Tell me!"

Lisa let out a heavy breath. "Okay, so Alyssa said Chantal broke up with Jon in a voicemail."

"What?"

"Jon told her Chantal left a message saying she was done with him and that he should date Alyssa because it was clear they had feelings for each other."

"Wait. What? That's what *I* said to him."

"Right... but you have to consider something else. You and Chantal sound exactly alike. Jon might have misheard the message and thought it was from her. That's why he flipped out on her and said he was going to date Alyssa."

Lisa's theory literally took Cathy's breath away.

"Did you say in the message that it was you?" Lisa asked.

Cathy frantically wracked her brain. "I was so nervous! I have no idea if I said my name or just started talking. I know I said I was returning his call, so he should have assumed it was me. Either way—even if he thought I was Chantal—I didn't say anything about breaking up!"

"Cathy, I think we figured it out," Lisa stated in a serious tone. "Think about this: Jon must have been feeling guilty for spending so much time with another girl. We could all see that he was pushing Chantal away. I bet his guilt led him to believe your message was a breakup because he was probably expecting her to break up with him. Then his anger took away his ability to reason, and he probably never even considered that the message could have been from you."

"Oh my gosh," Cathy said and then took a deep breath. She widened her eyes at the realization that she might have caused the entire mess.

"I didn't say anything to Alyssa about the message you left because here are my thoughts: Chantal is finally happy; if she finds out that Jon didn't mean to break up with her, she might consider letting him back into her life, and he's toxic."

"Holy crap. I can't believe I might have broken them up!" Cathy cried in dismay. Even though she despised the way Jon had been treating Chantal, she would never have intentionally come between them.

"You believe things happen for a reason, right?"

Cathy swallowed the large lump in her throat. "I believe God works everything together for the good of His followers."

"Look at how much happier Chantal is now than she was two months ago. Thinking about that makes me consider that perhaps what you believe is true."

"So, if that's how it all went down, then Jon probably said he was dating Alyssa because of what my message said, and Alyssa had nothing to do with it at all."

"Right," Lisa agreed. "So, what do we do? Do we let Alyssa lose her best friend for no reason or do we say something and risk Chantal getting mixed back up with Jon?"

"I hate this!" Cathy exclaimed.

"Chantal cut all of Jon's friends out of her life, so she probably won't hear his side of the story. If she were to find out the truth and reach out to him, he would try to get back together with her. He told Chris that he understands why she broke up with him, and that he can finally see how much he hurt her."

"I don't want Jon *anywhere* near my sister," Cathy stated emphatically.

"Me either. I want her and Andy to become boyfriend and girlfriend."

"So, we shouldn't mention what we think to anyone," Cathy proposed. "I won't even tell Jason. Don't tell Chris. We can buy time and see how long it takes for everyone else to figure it out. Maybe by then Chantal will love Andy more than Jon and not even care."

"I think it's in everyone's best interest if we keep quiet about our theory," Lisa agreed, "but we have to do something for Alyssa."

"I'll become friends with her again, and if Chantal questions me about it, I'll tell her that I don't think she hooked up with Jon."

"Will she get mad at you?" Lisa asked.

"I don't know. I mean, she knows I'm dating Jason and that he's friends with her, so she must expect that I'll run into her at some point," Cathy reasoned.

"Jason will figure it out," Lisa predicted. "He's too smart not to."

"Even if he knew, I doubt he'd tell Jon. He thinks Jon is a drama queen, and he wants Chantal to stay far away from him."

"Then maybe you should tell Jay so he doesn't figure it out and think you were hiding it from him."

Cathy let out a heavy breath. "It won't take long for him to figure it out—especially if I become friends with Alyssa again."

"Tell him, but tell him not to tell anyone. I won't say a word to Chris, Alyssa, or anyone we know. We can keep this between the three of us and cross our fingers that no one else figures it out."

"Okay," Cathy agreed. "I just want Chantal to be happy."

"Then we're doing the right thing," Lisa said.

"I'll call Jay. Why don't you ask Alyssa if she wants to hang out with us next weekend? Tell her that I believe her, and that I'm sorry I doubted her."

"She'll be happy," Lisa said. "Everyone will be."

Cathy was full of mixed emotions. She hated the idea of hiding something from Chantal; however, she loathed the possibility of Jon coming back into her sister's life. She knew Jason would help her sort through her feelings, so she called him as soon as she hung up with Lisa.

"But if Jon thought Chantal broke up with *him*, then why did he call her that night to break up with *her*?" Jason asked once Cathy finished explaining everything to him.

"He didn't. She called him when she got home from the mall, and he flipped out on her."

"Oh!" Jason cried. "That makes sense! What did your message say, again? That you thought he and Alyssa had feelings for each other?"

"Yeah, and that he should be dating her."

"Ahhh... so he took that as Chantal breaking up with him. Then she called him—not knowing any of this—and, out of spite, he said he was going to go out with Alyssa. So, neither one of them actually broke up with the other," Jason reasoned.

"Yeah. Something like that."

"That makes a lot of sense."

Cathy let out a heavy breath. "Here's the dilemma: Alyssa lost two of her close friends over nothing, and I feel horrible about it. I want Chantal to know that Alyssa didn't backstab her, but if Chantal were to become friends with Alyssa again, she would find out that Jon thought she broke up with him in a voicemail. She knows I left him an angry message that day. She would figure out that he mistook me for her and that they never meant to break up with each other. The thought of her giving Jon another chance horrifies me."

"Yikes!" Jason cried. "Letting Jon back into her life would mess things up with Andy."

"Right. So, what do I do? If our theory is true, then I broke them up! That's horrible!"

Jason laughed. "I think it's actually a blessing in disguise. It's exactly what they both needed. Jon wasn't treating her right, and she was becoming a doormat."

"True, but I feel bad. I mean, clearly, she's way better off without him, but I never would have deliberately broken them up."

"You did her a favor," Jason assured her. "If I were you, I wouldn't say a word about your theory to her. Let her be happy with Andy. Let Jon figure out his crap. If Andy and Chantal break up down the road and Jon's in a better place, tell her your theory, but for now, I think you should protect her from him."

"Lisa wants me to keep it between the three of us. I just don't know what to do about Alyssa."

"Alyssa did nothing wrong," Jason said. "You can become friends with her again even if Chantal doesn't."

"I just feel bad because Chantal thinks Jon left her for Alyssa. Even if I tell Chantal Alyssa never hooked up with Jon, she will still feel like I'm befriending her competition. My sister isn't a jealous person, but what happened really hurt her."

"That's why we have to do everything in our power to keep Chantal away from Jon," Jason stated.

"So, should I not hang out with Alyssa? I already told Lisa to make plans for us."

"Alyssa's one of my good friends. Chantal will understand if you end up hanging out with her," Jason reasoned. "Just tell her that you honestly don't believe she is to blame for Jon's behavior."

Cathy sighed. "Okay. I just hate keeping things from my sister."

"You're doing it for her own good," Jason assured her.

Cathy let out a heavy breath. "I fear this is going to come back to bite me."

"You just have a strong conscience. You're doing nothing wrong. *So what* if you have a theory and don't mention it to Chantal? You're not tricking her into anything. If your theory is true, the miscommunication was Jon's fault—not yours."

"True. I guess that makes me feel a little better," Cathy said, appreciating Jason's perspective.

"Great. Do you want to come over my house tomorrow? I have to stay after school for a little while, but I should be home by four."

"I'll ask my mom and call you back before I go to bed."

"Sounds good!" Jason exclaimed. "Love you."

"Love you, too."

CHAPTER 48

O VER THE NEXT FEW months, Cathy and Jason's relationship continued to strengthen. When summer arrived, Jason's family began spending most weekends at their beach house in Newport, and Cathy was invited each time. She cherished her time spent with Jason's family. They were warm, entertaining, and extremely generous. The Davids boys all made friends easily, so they had a good-sized crew to hang out with in Rhode Island. It was quickly becoming the best summer of Cathy's life.

Chantal and Andy were also growing closer. Without Cathy around on the weekends, Chantal was left to spend most of her time with Andy and his friends. As the summer progressed, Chantal began to feel more and more comfortable around his "boys"—Bobby Ryan, Jeff Brooke, and Adam Case. She appreciated that drugs were never involved in their plans. Katherine and Leslie began dating Bobby and Adam respectively, so they also hung out frequently. However, because Katherine and Leslie were Alyssa and Jon's friends from MLMS, Chantal was hesitant to befriend them.

Meanwhile, Lisa and Chris were facing some challenges: because Andy was Lisa's best friend, she wanted to spend time with him and Chantal, but because Jon was Chris's best friend, Chris felt doing so would betray Jon. Chris told Lisa it would have been different "if Chantal hadn't broken up with Jon for Andy." Lisa knew that was not the case, but she could not make that argument without exposing her and Cathy's theory.

Therefore, Lisa was forced to split her time between Chris's friends and her own friends from school. With Cathy and Jason in Newport and Bryan preoccupied with Courtney, Lisa and Chris ended up spending a significant amount of time with Alyssa and Jon. This brought Lisa and Alyssa closer but unfortunately put more space between her and Chantal.

Ironically, by cutting Alyssa out of her life, Chantal brought Alyssa and Jon even closer. By early August—three months after the infamous breakup—it became clear that romantic feelings were developing between Jon and Alyssa. However, also that month, an atrocity occurred that shifted everyone's focus.

Late one evening, Lisa's father was on his way home from work when a drunk driver crossed lanes and struck his vehicle head-on. Mr. Ankerman was in a coma for three days without brain activity before Lisa's oldest brother, JC, made the decision to cut life support. That day, Lisa's world came crashing down. JC, at age twenty-two, was forced to forgo law school, settle their father's estate, and stay in Montgomery as Lisa's legal guardian. The grief Lisa experienced made everything else in her life seem trivial, including her relationship with Chris. She broke up with him before school started so she could take time to grieve without the pressure of having to be his girlfriend.

Cathy and Jason came back from Rhode Island to a whirlwind. It was hard for Cathy to process how much had changed over that summer. She made comforting Lisa her priority, and Jason granted her the space to do so. Andy and Chantal also put their efforts towards helping Lisa heal. Nevertheless, the beginning of eighth grade was a dark time for Cathy's group of friends.

CHAPTER 49

IN EARLY SEPTEMBER, IT became public knowledge that Jon and Alyssa had officially become a couple. This only solidified Chantal's belief that Jon had broken up with her for Alyssa and that Alyssa had backstabbed her. Cathy was surprised by the news and could not fathom how a brother-sister-like friendship had turned into a romance. It made Cathy question if Jon had, in fact, broken up with her sister for Alyssa. It also gave her reservations about being Alyssa's friend, until she saw Chris the following weekend.

"I'm not surprised by it at all," Chris said to Cathy and Jason, referring to Jon and Alyssa's relationship. "Jon is heartbroken over Chantal, and he's rebounding. Alyssa is upset over losing her, too. They're clinging to each other because they're hurt. They tried to reach out to Chantal a bunch of times. She only took one of Alyssa's calls and just hysterically accused her of hooking up with Jon."

Cathy glanced at Jason, wondering if he felt as queasy as she did. Their decision to not tell anyone about their theory was haunting her. Although she was thrilled to see Chantal happy with Andy, she felt bad for Alyssa—really bad.

"I don't blame Chantal," Jason stated flatly. "Jon told her he was going to go out with her best friend, and now he is doing just that. If he still loves her, then he's being stupid."

"I get why you're siding with Tal, but you weren't around to see how bad Jon took the breakup," Chris said. "When he found out Lisa set Chantal back up with Andy, he lashed out at me. He made me promise not to hang out with Andy, which put tension between me and Lisa. It made for an awkward summer. You two were lucky to get out of Montgomery; you didn't get caught in the middle. Lisa and I would probably still be together if I had been willing to hang out with Andy's crew. She's leaning on them for support now, not me."

Jason sighed. "That sucks, dude. I'm sorry. Jon's a loose cannon. Drama follows him everywhere."

"Do you think there is *any* chance that he broke up with Chantal for Alyssa?" Cathy questioned Chris.

Chris shook his head. "No chance at all. He's full of regret. He knows he blew it. He was being an ass. Chantal didn't deserve any of that."

"So, you don't hate my sister?" Cathy asked.

"Of course not!" Chris exclaimed. "She's a sweetheart."

"That's a relief," Cathy said.

"Okay, but now I'm worried about Alyssa," Jason admitted. "If she falls for Jon, she's going to get hurt."

Chris shrugged. "She knows Jon better than any of us do. She'll proceed with caution."

"So, what now?" Jason asked. "Who's in our crew? Does Bryan ever hang out anymore?"

"I spent most of the summer with Lisa, Jon, Alyssa, Marc, and his friends," Chris replied. "Bryan hangs out with Courtney *constantly*. Leslie and Katherine started dating Andy's friends, so they haven't been around lately. It was a low-key summer, aside from all the heartbreak. Poor Lisa. Her dad...I can't believe it. First her mom leaves; then her dad gets killed. I don't know how she's functioning. I want to be there for her, but she's pushing me away."

"She thinks you chose Jon's feelings over hers," Cathy said. "She pulled back for that reason."

Chris sighed. "I tried my best to stay neutral, but I guess I did choose Jon's feelings over hers. I honestly had no idea it would be such a big deal to her if I didn't hang out with Andy."

"She hides her feelings well," Cathy remarked. "I'm going to spend as much time with her as I can, and I'll make sure she understands the amount of pressure Jon put on you."

"Thanks," Chris said. "It's going to take me a while to get over her."

"So, does Jon expect *me* not to spend time with Chantal and Andy?" Jason asked.

Chris laughed. "I don't think he expects anything from you. He knows you're fed up with him."

"Good!" Jason cried. "I'll try to loop Bryan back into the group. Maybe he'll finally let us meet Courtney."

"Ha. Fat chance!" Chris cried sarcastically. "She's not a partier. He thinks we'll scare her away."

"Cathy's not a partier, and we didn't scare her away," Jason retorted.

"That's true!" Chris laughed. "Cathy, why didn't we scare you away?"

Cathy cocked her head to the side in thought. "I guess because you're all so nice. Jason doesn't drink, and you're fine with that. I've never felt pressured to do anything I didn't want to do at your parties. You accept people as they are. Courtney would be lucky to meet you guys. Bryan's probably just afraid she'll like one of you more than him."

Chris laughed. "Who knows what that kid thinks? Where do you stand with Alyssa?"

"We were cool before the summer, but I haven't talked to her since she started going out with Jon," Cathy replied. "If you're sure there's no way he broke up with my sister for her, then I'm open to hanging out with her again."

"Jon swears Chantal broke up with him," Chris said, "and I believe him."

The pit in Cathy's stomach grew, and she knew for certain that Jon had mistaken her voicemail for Chantal's breakup message. "I'll reach out to Alyssa. If Katherine and Leslie are dating Andy's friends and Lisa is grieving, then she's probably in need of some female companionship."

"She could use a friend," Chris agreed.

Motivated by compassion, Cathy set off that day to befriend Alyssa. It was impossible at that time for anyone to foresee how grave the consequences of that decision would be. Cathy expected Chantal to be somewhat uncomfortable with their friendship, but she did not expect too much backlash. She informed Chantal that Alyssa did not hook up with Jon until *after* Chantal and Andy had become an official couple. She tried her best to defend Alyssa, but Chantal became irate. She stopped inviting Cathy places and ceased confiding in her. Cathy had never experienced the infamous "Chantal shut-out" until then. It drove a wedge between the twins and hurt Cathy deeply.

Soon after, she began to experience depression and anxiety, unlike anything she had ever known. When Cathy discussed the situation with her mother and Jason, they both assumed Chantal just needed more time to heal from her first heartbreak and that she would let Cathy back into her inner circle in due time. However, as eighth grade progressed, their paths continued to diverge.

CHAPTER 50

***

Present Day

ITTING ON THE BLEACHERS inside the gym, Jason watched as Chantal reacted to the story he had just shared with her. She took a deep breath. "Wait," she huffed while gaping at him. "Cathy didn't deliberately break up me and Jon?!"

Jason was taken aback by her question. "Of course not," he said in a perplexed manner. "You thought she broke you up?"

Chantal's green eyes were glazed with tears. Slowly, she nodded. "She became close with Alyssa after our breakup, and Lisa was so happy to see me with Andy. I heard at church that Jon was claiming he never broke up with me, so I convinced myself that Cathy, Alyssa, and Lisa had somehow plotted the breakup. I knew Cathy was mad at Jon, so it made sense. I assumed she pretended to be me and broke up with him."

Jason widened his eyes. "She would never have done something like that," he stated defensively and lowered his eyebrows. "Her relationship with you meant the world to her. Alyssa had nothing to do with any of it, and Lisa only wanted to see you treated right. Jon was being a jerk, and we wanted to protect you from him."

"I knew Cathy was somehow responsible," Chantal said. "I can't explain how I knew, but I knew. I guess...I guess...I assumed the worst. When Andy was in the hospital last fall, Jon came to visit me. When he mentioned I broke up with him in a voicemail, I completely forgot about the message Cathy left him on the day of our breakup. It never once crossed my mind. I automatically assumed she pretended to be me. I told him that. I told Alyssa that when I became friends with her again. I told a lot of people that," she admitted as her voice cracked.

"Why did you assume the worst?" Jason asked, searching Chantal's eyes. He had always thought of her as someone who saw the best in others.

Tears began seeping from Chantal's eyes. "Because Cathy was acting psychotic at the time," she replied, "to you, to me, to my parents, to everyone."

Jason swallowed the large lump in his throat and took a deep breath before speaking. "I know you're already late for cheer practice—"

"I can't go to practice like this," Chantal interrupted him and wiped tears from her eyes.

"Well, if you can hang out a little longer, I can tell you the rest of the story," Jason said compassionately. "It's going to be hard to hear, especially because yours and Cathy's relationship had a lot to do with it, but I think you should know the truth."

Chantal nodded. "Tell me. Don't hold anything back," she said. "Tell me why my sister turned into a narcissist and why she gave up on trying to fix our relationship. Tell me about the drugs—what they are and how they got a grip on her. Tell me everything."

"I will," Jason said, "and you'll finally understand why I am to blame for the shattered person Cathy is today."

Tears had continued streaming down Chantal's face. "I can't believe I assumed such horrible things," she expressed sadly. "It should have dawned on me that I was being judgmental. Love sees no evil, but when I looked at Cathy, all I saw was evil." Chantal took a deep breath. She looked as though the wind had been knocked out of her.

CHAPTER 51

WHILE LUKE AND CATHY were still outside on the balcony, Taylor picked his iPhone up off the coffee table. Navigating to Instagram, he opened Luke's profile. Months earlier, Marc had blocked Taylor from all of his social media accounts, but thankfully Luke frequently posted pictures with Marc and their friends.

Taylor had recently noticed a girl beside Marc in a lot of pictures, and he assumed Marc was hooking up with her—Marc didn't usually "date" anyone. When Cathy walked through the door, Taylor thought she looked familiar. Only after Luke introduced them did he correlate her with Jason. As they were talking, Taylor began wondering why Luke was hanging out with his little brother's ex-girlfriend and why Cathy seemed so uncomfortable. Then something occurred to him.

Scrolling to a picture from the previous night, Taylor saw Luke in his MLH hockey jersey with his girlfriend Missy, his brother Matt, Marc, and a girl who looked just like Cathy. Knowing Cathy was a twin, Taylor checked to see who was tagged: @ckagelli99. After touching the tag, he was brought to a profile that, indeed, said Cathaleen. As he scrolled through her page, he saw pictures of her and Marc that dated back to Christmas. Knowing how against drugs Marc was, Taylor was surprised he would go out with Cathy. She was pretty, but even Taylor knew she and Jason had experimented with worse drugs than weed or alcohol.

As Taylor closed out of Instagram, flashbacks of the last time he saw

Marc infiltrated his mind. He could not believe he had let his youngest brother see him in such a state of weakness. After enduring a week and a half of withdrawal pains and feeling like his skin was crawling for nearly a month, Taylor never wanted to see an opiate again, and he certainly didn't want anyone he knew getting mixed up in them. The amount of guilt he harbored over selling Xanax and Vicodin to Luke was overwhelming. He was fearful that Luke had gotten numerous kids from Montgomery into benzos and painkillers.

After much soul-searching, Taylor realized that his drug problem had begun long before his injury. Since his freshman year in college, he had thought that sporadically dabbling with substances such as coke and molly equated to harmless fun. Because he formed no addictions prior to his injury, he had perceived no danger in partying during the offseason. In hindsight, Taylor could see that using drugs warped his values, causing him to prioritize his social life over his football career. Instead of transferring colleges as a sophomore, he had chosen to remain at Northeastern, simply because he was comfortable there—his professors, coaches, and friends adored him. In retrospect, he loathed himself for that decision. Taylor was extremely ashamed of the person he had become, and with newfound clarity, he was in awe of the way drugs had not only skewed his perception, but also changed his ambitions.

A moment later, Cathy and Luke came back inside the apartment, interrupting Taylor's thoughts. At the sight of Cathy, he felt awkward. He did not want Marc or anyone in his family to find out that he was still dealing drugs. Four months prior, Taylor had used his father's money as planned: to pay off his supplier and move away from the negative influences in his life. His supplier, however, had put an enormous amount of pressure on him to sell another batch, saying that would allot him time to find another distributer at the college level. Taylor knew his supplier was well-connected to criminals who would not think twice about taking him out, so he agreed to sell one more stash—free of opiates—out of fear alone. However, after each sale, Taylor felt guiltier and guiltier.

"So, I talked Cathy into taking the Xanax you found," Luke announced before sitting down on the couch.

As Taylor watched Cathy's green eyes drop to the floor, his heart began to pound. "You know what? I think what I found is the stuff my doctor prescribed to help me sleep. You probably don't want this, Cathy," he said and peered at her, hoping she would refuse the drug. He wasn't lying; last month, his doctor prescribed him a low dose of Xanax to mitigate his insomnia.

Cathy let out what sounded like a sigh of relief. "It's probably for the best," she said and sat down beside Luke. She looked up at Taylor and spread her pale lips into a slight smile.

"So, we are thinking of going to lunch somewhere on Broadway. Want to come?" Luke asked.

"I'm good but thanks," Taylor replied. "I actually have some business to take care of at Northeastern this afternoon."

"Oh, no way, man? That's great. Are you thinking of going back?" Luke inquired.

Taylor shrugged. "I have to straighten out my transcript and see what my options are. I doubt Northeastern will readmit me, but I'm going to talk with my old advisor and find out what's possible. I'm looking into transferring, but I think my grades from last year are going to be problematic."

"I'm sure you'll be able to figure something out," Luke remarked.

"I've got to do whatever it takes to get back on the field. I'm eligible for one more season of D-I ball. That's it."

Luke smiled. "Marc would be so happy to know you're thinking about school again. I would tell him, but he probably shouldn't know we saw each other today."

Taylor laughed awkwardly. "Yeah... I'll tell him soon. He's been waiting way too long for me to get my act together."

Luke cocked his head to the side and widened his hazel eyes. "Are you not selling painkillers anymore?"

Taylor assumed Luke had finally realized he was clean. "No, man. You don't want those things anyway—trust me."

To Taylor's surprise, Luke did not look at all disappointed. In fact, he seemed happy to hear the news. Cathy certainly looked relieved. Perhaps it was a gift that two of Marc's closest companions were there to hear about the positive changes Taylor had been making to his lifestyle.

CHAPTER 52

A T BOSTON COLLEGE, MARC was going over the current roster with one of his future coaches when a middle-aged man, wearing a blue collared shirt and khakis, walked into the office. Marc assumed he was a professor until he asked for Marc directly.

"I'll let you two talk," the coach said and quickly scurried out of the room, closing the door behind him. Marc was perplexed. He gazed warily at the man, who was taking a seat across from him at the table.

"Hi, Marc," the man said. "I'm Detective Roth of the BPD."

Marc took a deep breath. "Is my brother dead?" he asked in a somber tone.

"No," Detective Roth replied and shook his head.

Marc felt the color return to his face as he let out a heavy sigh of relief.

"You are right to be concerned about him, though," the detective commented. "I need you to get a message to him." He pulled a black cell phone out of his briefcase and handed it to Marc. "Tell him, we know he wants out of the game, and we can make that happen. Have him call the number programmed in that phone when he's ready to discuss his options. Tell him he needs to use great discretion and that he cannot use that phone in public or for any other calls."

"Why are you giving this to me?" Marc asked. "I haven't spoken to Taylor in months."

"He's likely being watched by criminals who can't see him make contact with anyone on the police force," Detective Roth said. "That would put his life in danger, but they won't think anything of you stopping by his apartment."

"He's being watched?" Marc asked and swallowed deeply. "How bad is it?"

"From one Eagle to another," Detective Roth said and raised his eyebrows, "really bad."

Marc's heart began to pound against his muscular chest and his throat went completely dry. "I'll do whatever you need me to do," he pledged in a solemn tone.

"The less involved you have to be, the better," Detective Roth said. "You and your brother Jordan are good kids, and you don't want anything to do with the mess Taylor has entangled himself in. We just need you to open the line of communication for us, and then your role is done. Okay?"

Marc nodded, bewildered that the detective knew about him and his family.

"Taylor will want to talk to us," Detective Roth said. "He's clean and ready."

Marc raised his eyebrows. "He is? How do you know?"

Detective Roth smiled. "The less you know, the better. Can you get that phone to him today?"

Marc nodded. "Yeah, I can call him when I leave here and ask to drop by. If he's home, I'll go right over."

"The sooner, the better," the detective stated. He reached across the table to shake Marc's hand before standing up to leave the room.

"How did you know I was here?" Marc questioned him.

"My boss set up your meeting," Detective Roth replied. "You're important to this school."

Marc stared at the detective thoughtfully. How could his importance to BC's football team have anything to do with Taylor being a drug dealer? He could tell from the detective's somber tone, however, that getting the cell phone to Taylor was imperative.

GRIPPED PART 2 PREVIEW

March of 2018

TAYLOR DUNKIN SIGHED AFTER shutting his front door behind Luke Davids and Cathy Kagelli. When Luke asked to stop by earlier that afternoon, Taylor feared he would want to buy drugs. After sending Luke off with molly and cocaine, Taylor hoped Marc would not find out about their rendezvous. He knew Luke would also want to keep it a secret, but he feared Cathy would divulge the information. More than anything, Taylor wanted to make things right with his brother. The dissension between Marc and himself bothered Taylor more than any other consequence of his drug addiction.

As he made his way toward his bedroom, he pulled his iPhone out of his pocket to check the time: 2:24 P.M.; he would have to leave for his meeting at Northeastern in about twenty minutes. As he entered his bedroom, his phone began to vibrate in his hand as a call came through from his cousin Chris.

"Hello?" Taylor answered.

"Hey, T," Chris replied. "Do you have a minute?"

"Sure, buddy. What's up?" he asked.

"Are you coming home for Easter this weekend?"

Taylor's heart sank. "I don't think so, man. Sorry."

"I was afraid you were going to say that," Chris replied downheartedly. "Well... my parents are hosting this year, and I just wanted to make sure you knew you were invited. We miss you."

Taylor sighed as he sat down on his bed. "I miss you guys, too."

"Can I be honest with you?"

"Of course," Taylor replied, wondering what was on Chris's mind.

"It's hard to believe you're clean when you don't ever come home."

I should have expected that.

"If everything was really fine, I think you'd at least come home for holidays," Chris added.

"I promise that I'm sober," Taylor stated. "Things are just complicated. I would come home if I could."

"But you can," Chris pressed. "Just because you're in a fight with Marc doesn't mean no one else wants to see you. Marc is wrong to blame you for other people's drug problems."

"No, he's not."

"T, you didn't make anyone do anything. If you didn't sell to Luke, I would have found someone else to buy from. Stop blaming yourself for other people's poor decisions."

"The only thing that makes me feel better is the fact that you're sober," Taylor admitted. "I exposed you to terrible things—you and so many other people. You have no idea what it feels like to live with so much shame."

"No, but I have some idea. I used to blame myself for getting my friends into drugs. Most of them, thankfully, are on better paths now, but a lot of damage was done before I sobered up."

"It's small in comparison to the damage I have caused, and you would never have gotten into drugs if I hadn't continuously thrown parties at your house."

"You don't know that," Chris retorted. "My life was missing something, and I thought partying was the answer. I would have gotten into trouble without your help."

"Partying is definitely not the answer."

"No, it's not. Our lives prove that much, but blame is a vicious cycle: you blame yourself for getting me into drugs; I blame myself for getting Jason messed up; Jay blames himself for getting his ex-girlfriend all screwed up; and I'm pretty sure she's living with a lot of self-loathing. It never ends. But we can't keep thinking like that because it's a farce. When you told me that you feel responsible for my issues, it set me free from a significant amount of guilt—but *not* because you are to blame."

Chris's words caught Taylor off guard.

"I never blamed you for my drug problem because I knew I had made the conscious decision to dabble," Chris continued. "The thought of you being responsible for that was preposterous to me, which made me realize I was not responsible for Jason, Jon, or Bryan's past drug use. They all made their own decisions for their own reasons—just like I did."

Taylor was somewhat stunned by the wisdom flowing from his younger cousin's mouth. Recently, every time they spoke, Taylor walked away with a better perspective. The recovery meetings, church, and Bible studies that Chris had been attending since he got sober were changing his life, and that motivated Taylor to attend AA with his father. However, he felt an enormous amount of guilt each time he went because he was still, technically, a drug dealer.

Chris was now seven months sober. He had reached out to Taylor a few months back to share his story. Chris took no credit for his recovery but instead attributed it to the strength he found in God. What he said reminded Taylor of what he had learned at Al-Anon and what his parents had always taught him and his brothers: if you feed your spirit, you will be able to conquer your flesh. Taylor's spirit had been crushed by failure and deep-seeded regret. Numbing his emotions with drugs, instead of facing his problems, had driven him to a very dangerous place.

"You're allowing shame and regret to keep you from coming home, but the truth is every day you remain estranged hurts us more and more," Chris said. "What's done is done. Not coming home only makes the damage worse. Everyone who loves you just wants to forget about the past and move forward with you back in their lives."

Taylor let out a heavy sigh and glanced at the clock on his desk. "I appreciate what you're saying, and I want to come home soon. I really do. I have to head out to a meeting now, but I'll call you tonight, and we can talk more."

"All right. Don't forget," Chris said before ending the call.

As Taylor set down his phone, he dwelled on his cousin's words. He hated the idea of causing his family more pain by keeping to himself, but after realizing the damage he had caused, he had begun to believe everyone would be better off without him. It scared him that he had unwittingly hurt so many people. He was keeping himself away from his family for their own protection. It was a catch twenty-two, though, because protecting them from potential pain was causing them actual pain.

Despite all of the thoughts running through his mind, Taylor knew he had to focus his attention on his academic record before going to his meeting at Northeastern. He sat down at his computer and opened up a PDF file of his transcript. As he looked over his grades, a pit formed in his stomach. He was so embarrassed. How was he going to explain having a 3.4 cumulative GPA through his junior year and then earning a 1.8 average as a senior?

He closed his eyes. *You have to do this*, he said to himself. *You have to try to fix things.*

After opening his eyes, he logged into his bank account online and checked his balance. His father had continued to deposit money into his account to put toward his rent each month, even though Taylor had asked him not to. He did not have the heart to tell his dad that he had made over $50,000 selling drugs and that he did not need any money. He dreaded his family ever finding out how big of a drug dealer he had been.

In November, his father flushed approximately $5,000 worth of drugs down the toilet. Months later, Taylor wished he never let on to how costly the act had been. His father knew nothing about the street value of cocaine or Percocet, and Taylor wished in hindsight that he had kept his mouth shut. He hated taking his father's money, but he was too much of a coward to tell him the truth. The money sitting in Taylor's bank account, safe, storage unit, and safety deposit box did not make up for any of the destruction drugs brought into his life. He would have traded every cent for healthy relationships with his family.

The ironic thing was Taylor did not begin selling drugs to make money. He liked the idea of getting the expensive pills he wanted dirt cheap and being able to sell to his friends at a discount. When he agreed to start dealing, he did so because he wanted to make it easier for people he knew to get their hands on "fun substances" like cocaine, molly, and painkillers. He never imagined how quickly word would spread around campus or how time-consuming dealing drugs would become. Attending class every day and studying were nearly impossible when customers were constantly looking for product. Without football as a motivation to keep his grades high, Taylor quickly lost sight of the big picture. Thoughts such as *"why should I go to class to learn about marketing when I'm already a successful salesman?"* motivated him to hit the snooze button far too many mornings, and unfortunately, he did not see the fault in his thought process until his trimester GPA slipped below the allowed minimum.

Failing out of his major was his first wakeup call. His second one came in the form of withdrawal pains—prior to which he had not realized he even had an addiction. Recognizing that he was dependent on a substance horrified him enough to begin detoxing. His final wakeup call was the loss of his relationship with Marc. In fact, Taylor had not touched a painkiller since

Marc stormed out of his apartment in November.

After logging out of his computer, Taylor rose from his chair, grabbed his keys, and headed off in his Jeep toward Huntington Avenue. He had feared for months that administrators at Northeastern had heard about his drug abuse, drug-dealing, or both. Therefore, he was surprised to get an email from his former coach earlier that week, checking in on him. He informed Taylor that Northeastern made the shocking decision to terminate its football program and that he would be relocating to another university—location to be determined. He encouraged Taylor to set up a meeting with his advisor to see if he was transfer eligible; he wanted to help Taylor get back on the field and preferably at his new place of employment.

Taylor's father always told him and his brothers that if they did the right thing, God would send the right opportunities their way. Taylor hoped that this was one of those opportunities. He believed he was doing "the right thing" in many areas of his life, but he knew his drug-dealing days had to come to an end if he wanted to move forward. The sickening feeling in his stomach when he sold drugs to Luke that afternoon had only served to solidify that notion.

Cathy Kagelli and Luke Davids decided to eat lunch at a sushi restaurant one block down from Taylor's South Boston apartment. Although Luke had generously ordered an array of Cathy's favorite dishes, she had no appetite. Her stomach was in knots over the thought of seeing Marc. How was she going to keep from him that she had seen Taylor? She couldn't; her conscience was not going to allow her to do that, and she knew it.

"Why aren't you eating anything?" Luke questioned her as he put down his chopsticks and eyed her in a concerned manner.

"I just don't feel that well," Cathy replied, hoping he wouldn't press the issue.

"Marc didn't get you pregnant, did he?" Luke asked and raised his eyebrows at her expectantly.

Cathy rolled her eyes. "We haven't slept together," she stated in an unamused manner. "Why do you Davids boys always think people who hook up have sex?"

Luke laughed. "Jason and I may have different reasons for assuming that, but I have it on pretty good authority that you're not a virgin."

"I hate you sometimes," Cathy retorted and shook her head.

"Well, if you're not pregnant, then what's wrong with you?" Luke asked curiously.

Cathy assumed he was trying to get her to explain her odd behavior. Unlike Luke, Cathy hated talking about feelings. In their friendship, the female and male roles were a bit reversed: Luke was far more of a "pretty boy" than Cathy was a "girlie girl." Even though Luke was the captain of the varsity hockey team and known for winning fights, Cathy's conversations with him were similar to those had with her girlfriends. She assumed Luke was dying with curiosity over her and Marc's relationship, wanting to know if she was still in love with his brother Jason or if she had truly moved onto Marc. She honestly did not know the answer to that question. Marc was every girl at Montgomery Lake High's dream: a gifted athlete, smart, responsible, and caring, with a body that could be blasted on the cover of magazines and eyes as blue as the sky. However, Jason fit a similar description—at least since he got his life back together.

In the fall, Cathy and Jason went through a disastrous breakup, both hitting their rock bottoms. She had assumed since November that he hated her—until she received a note from him that morning. The letter was still in her pocket, and she looked forward to re-reading it and sorting out her feelings, alone. Luke was eyeing her expectantly, and Cathy knew she had to explain herself in some manner. "I don't want to lie to Marc," she blurted.

"About what?"

"About going to Taylor's!"

"You don't have to lie to him," Luke said, looking puzzled.

Cathy widened her eyes. "Uh, yeah I do unless you want him to find out Taylor sells you drugs."

"You don't have to say anything," Luke stated. "When we pick Marc up at BC, let me do all the talking. He'll ask what we did, and I'll tell him."

"You'll tell him?"

"I'll tell him everything except for the part about Taylor."

Cathy sighed with frustration. "Omitting information like that is not okay! It feels like lying; it puts space between people. My most healthy relationships are my most honest ones. Hiding things from people has brought too much destruction to my life. I am not going to risk losing Marc over this."

Luke let out a heavy breath. "Fine. Tell him. He probably already knows."

"You think?"

Luke shrugged. "He could."

"Wouldn't he have confronted you about it?"

"I don't know," Luke replied. "Marc's weird about his family. If he got mad at me about it, people would find out, and that would make Taylor look bad."

"People know he's in a fight with Taylor," Cathy remarked. "That makes Taylor look bad."

Luke shook his head. "It's not the same thing. Brothers fight. Best friends usually don't. Everyone at our school knows Marc and I have a bromance. If we were to stop hanging out, people would notice and talk about it because they love to talk crap."

"Interesting," Cathy said and cocked her head to the side in thought. "Maybe that's why they had a falling out. Maybe Marc found out he was selling drugs to you and stopped talking to him."

"Maybe," Luke replied carelessly. "Like I said, Marc is super protective of his family. He hates Jordan and still doesn't say anything too bad about him."

"Um, other than that he 'tried to date-rape' Michelle Taylor!" Cathy cried, referring to MLH's homecoming queen—Marc's ex-girlfriend, for whom he was presumed to still have some feelings. Marc had not committed to a single girl, including Cathy, since his and Michelle's eighth-grade breakup. He had certainly hooked up with a fair share of girls, but he had called no one but Michelle his girlfriend.

"Everyone knows about what happened between Jordan and Michelle at Chris's house," Luke said matter-of-factly. "That's probably part of the reason why Marc is so weird about his family. He is the only Dunkin with an untarnished reputation."

"Jordan plays for Notre Dame. He's kind of famous," Cathy stated. "Aside from the few who actually believe he tried to date-rape Michelle, I'd say people think pretty highly of him."

"He's a good football player," Luke remarked. "No one will deny that, but I'm talking about what people in our town think. Marc's embarrassed by his brothers' off-field behavior—just like Matt and Jay are embarrassed by me."

Cathy laughed. "Matt's been embarrassed by both of you a million times. I bet he can't wait to go off to college and leave Montgomery."

Luke smirked. "He'll miss me," he said facetiously.

"So, you'd really be okay with me telling Marc that we saw Taylor?" Cathy questioned him.

Luke sighed. "He'll probably take a swing at me, but if keeping it from him is going to tear you up, tell him."

"Thanks," Cathy said, remembering why she adored Luke so much. Even though he was often criticized for being a reckless and spoiled rich kid, he was as warmhearted as his younger brother.

CHECK OUT THE REST OF THE GRIPPED SERIES

Gripped Part 2: Blindsided

Fourteen-year-old Chris Dunkin is known for being the life of the party and everyone's favorite friend. Despite his amicable nature, he carries around deep-seated pain from his childhood that he frequently numbs with alcohol and drugs.

After hosting a party, Chris awakes with a strange vibe running through his body and no recollection of the previous night. When he learns the horrifying truth of what his night entailed, the trajectory of his life is changed forever.

Gripped Part 3: The Fallout

After a near-death experience, Chris Dunkin begins surrounding himself with positive influences and putting his efforts towards living a clean lifestyle. However, the night before school starts, his best friend Jason convinces him to host a party that shows Chris more about himself than he actually wants to know.

Meanwhile, Marc Dunkin has received word from a detective that his oldest brother Taylor is a person of interest in a highly confidential case headed by the Boston Police Department. They know Taylor's clean; they know he wants out of the game; and they want to help make that happen. However, their "help" will come at a cost—one that may put Taylor and his entire family in grave danger.

Taylor is trying to get his life back in order after an opiate addiction wreaked havoc on his once promising athletic future. Getting clean was a difficult feat, but breaking free from the Bilotti crime ring will present an even greater challenge.

Gripped Part 4: Smoke & Mirrors

Taylor Dunkin is used to high stakes. As an NCAA star quarterback, he performed under pressure to lead his team to victory, but his football career came to an abrupt halt when an injury sent him spiraling down a dark hole of pain, depression, and addiction. Now he finds himself playing a game with even higher stakes because his life, his reputation, and the safety of everyone he loves are all on the line.

Taylor's two younger brothers, Jordan and Marc, have been at odds for years, but they are brought together to decipher the mysterious clues Taylor is leaving regarding his whereabouts. As secrets are revealed, the Dunkin boys' relationships will be changed forever.

In Taylor's weakest moment, he made a deal with the devil, and now there is a reckoning. But who will pay the price?

Gripped Part 5: Taylor's Story
Taylor Dunkin is missing.

The last message Jordan Dunkin receives from Taylor leads him to Taylor's abandoned Jeep. Each of Taylor's family members holds a piece of the puzzle, and as the Dunkins begin putting the details together, they are awakened to the possibility they may never see Taylor again.

No one can find Missy Kent.

Missy's boyfriend Luke Davids last saw her dancing with their friends at a nightclub, but she hasn't responded to anyone's texts or calls for hours.

Everything is connected.

Taylor and Missy's friends are dangerously close to learning the truth, but their ignorance might be the only thing keeping them safe. Every clue is leading them closer to peril.

The fifth book in the Gripped series moves through details at a thrilling pace. Secrets are revealed and lives are at stake. Taylor, Missy, their friends, and their families must figure out who they can trust before it's too late.

IF YOU ENJOYED *GRIPPED,* CHECK OUT
MONTGOMERY LAKE HIGH

Montgomery Lake High #1: The Right Person

Growing up in the shadow of two NFL-destined cousins, Chris Dunkin has high hopes for his own future in football. However, a drug addiction threatens to destroy everything he has worked hard to attain. When Chris meets Courtney Angeletti—the mayor's straightedge Christian daughter—he believes she could be the source of inspiration he needs to overcome his destructive lifestyle. Courtney, however, has other ideas.

The desire to rebel has been tugging on Courtney's heartstrings for some time, and Chris's "bad-boy" reputation draws her to him like a moth to a flame. After all, he is a central part of the most popular clique in her high school. Will Chris pull Courtney away from her faith or will Courtney inspire him to overcome his rebellious lifestyle?

Montgomery Lake High #2: When Darkness Tries to Hide

A powerful supercell is spawning above Montgomery Lake High School, while a separate storm is brewing in its halls. The question is which one should Cathy Kagelli, Jason Davids, and their friends fear the most?

Montgomery Lake High #3: The Aftermath

At age fifteen, Jason Davids appears to have it all: high grades, popular friends, a beautiful girlfriend, and nearly any worldly thing that promises enjoyment at his disposal. Despite this, there is a persistent emptiness inside his heart. After failing to fill the void with achievements, relationships, and illicit substances, Jason finds himself intrigued by Jessie: a rather quiet girl, who is the daughter of a local pastor. How is it possible that she stands for everything his lifestyle opposes yet possesses the one thing he has been searching for all along?

Montgomery Lake High #4: The Battle for Innocence

Jon Anderson and Chantal Kagelli are trying to live moral lives, but temptations are plaguing them in and out of school. Will they continue to be lights in their best friends' lives or will they get pulled into the darkness?

Montgomery Lake High #5: The Forces Within

After being trapped inside his own body, unable to communicate with anyone but his own thoughts, Andy Rosetti finally wakes up from the coma that controlled his life for one month. But upon awakening, Andy finds himself and his friends in an unfamiliar setting: a mansion riddled with secret passages and supernatural forces. As his friends fall prey to the entities surrounding them, Andy must figure out if the darkness lies within the mansion's walls or within the people surrounding him.

ABOUT THE AUTHOR

College counselor, award-winning author, and entrepreneur Stacy Padula of Plymouth, Massachusetts has accrued years of experience working with adolescents as an educational consultant, as well as a mentor, life coach, and youth group leader. She is the author of eleven Young Adult novels. Her first novel, "The Right Person," was published in 2010. In 2011, "When Darkness Tries to Hide" was published, and it was followed by "The Aftermath" in 2013. In 2014, both "The Battle for Innocence" and "The Forces Within" were released, and in 2015, all five books hit the shelves of Barnes & Noble. For Stacy, it was a dream come true to see her books for sale in the popular, mainstream bookstore! In 2016, Barnes & Noble chose Stacy to be a featured author for its teen book festival. In 2019, she released a new book series titled "Gripped," that takes place in the same "world" as Montgomery Lake High but focuses on different main characters. "Gripped Part 1: The Truth We Never Told" was released in February 2019, and "Gripped Part 2: Blindsided" was released in July 2019. "Gripped Part 3: The Fallout" was released in November 2019, and "Gripped Part 4: Smoke & Mirrors" was released in May 2020. In 2019, Stacy Padula also wrote her first screenplay, an adaptation of her novel "The Aftermath" and worked on writing a pilot for "Gripped" which caught the attention of Hollywood producers. The "Gripped" series is currently being adapted for TV by Emmy-winning producer Mark Blutman. In 2020, Stacy began writing a third book series with NBA Coach Brett Gunning. Geared towards children ages three through eight, Stacy and Brett's soon-to-be-released "On The Right Path" book series has been endorsed by Joel Osteen, Mike D'Antoni, and Kevin McHale as a series that belongs in every school, library, and household.

Stacy was featured in Marquis Who's Who in America (2018, 2019, & 2020) for excellence in literature and education, Marquis Who's Who in the World (2018, 2019, & 2020), and Cambridge Who's Who for Young Professionals (2009). In 2018, she was awarded the Albert Nelson Lifetime

Achievement Award, and in 2019, the International Association of Top Professionals (IAOTP of New York, NY) chose Stacy Padula as its "Top Educational Consultant of the Year." Then in 2020, she was named "Empowered Woman of the Year" by IAOTP. Each of her novels have risen to best seller status in a variety of categories on Amazon from 2010-Present. From February through March of 2019, "Gripped Part 1" was the #1 New Release on Amazon Kindle in its category. In November of 2019, "Gripped Part 3" was the #1 New Release on Amazon in Paperback and on Kindle in 3 different genres. In May and June of 2020, "Gripped Part 4" became the #1 New Release on Amazon in multiple genres as well. In November of 2020, Stacy was named a "Social Impact Hero" by Authority Magazine for her support of animal rescues through her publishing company. That month, she was also chosen to be featured on the cover of T.I.P. Magazine, an international business publication. In April of 2021, "On The Right Path" because the #1 New Release on Amazon in its genre. In June of 2021, Stacy was featured on the famous Reuters Building in Times Square as Empowered Woman of the Year.

Background: Stacy grew up in Pembroke, Massachusetts and graduated from Silver Lake Regional High School. She was a Presidential Scholar and on the Dean's List at Wentworth, where she studied Architectural Engineering and Interior Design. After graduation, she worked at an architecture firm in Boston from 2006-2008. Although she enjoyed her work, she felt something was missing-she wanted to spend more time helping people grow academically, personally, and spiritually. For close to a year, she split her time between tutoring, writing, and working at a design firm in Plymouth. When she fell in love with tutoring, she left the A&D industry completely and took a full-time position with a private education company in Dover, Massachusetts. She attained tutoring certification in 2009 through The International Tutor Association. Her career took off, and within one year, she was promoted to Director. Stacy knew she had found her niche! During her eight years with that company, she received multiple promotions and held a variety of titles, including Manager of Curriculum & Instruction and Director of Operations. In 2016, Stacy founded South Shore College Consulting & Tutoring. Then in 2019, she founded

Briley & Baxter Publications—a publishing company that uses part of its monthly proceeds to support animal rescues. Stacy is currently enrolled in the University of Pennsylvania Wharton School's online Entrepreneurship Specialization to pursue her passion for business. In her spare time, she enjoys skiing, taking online classes, following the stock market, attending Bruins games, playing fantasy sports, reading about psychology, hosting Bible studies, taking her dogs to the beach, and spending time with her family, husband Tim, and friends.

CONNECT WITH US!

Gripped's Instagram @gripped.book.series
Stacy's Instagram @author_stacypadula
Cathy's Instagram @ckagelli99
Chantal's Instagram @chantal_kagelli
Jason's Instagram @jds_on
Lisa's Instagram @lisa_ankerman99
Chris's Instagram @dunkin_85
Luke's Instagram @lukedavids97
Alyssa's Instagram @alyssa_kelly02
Stacy's Twitter @thegrippedbooks
www.stacyapadula.com
www.brileybaxterbooks.com
www.highambition.org

Did You Enjoy Gripped?
If you loved this book, please leave a review on Amazon!

CPSIA information can be obtained
at www.ICGtesting.com
Printed in the USA
BVHW072314060622
639031BV00007B/96